Odd Ducks

Odd Ducks

Stories

Patricia Lawson

BkMk Press
University of Missouri-Kansas City

BkMk Press
University of Missouri-Kansas City
5101 Rockhill Road
Kansas City, MO 64110

Executive Editor: Christie Hodgen
Managing Editor: Ben Furnish
Assistant Managing Editor: Cynthia Beard

Partial support for this project has been provided by the Missouri Arts
Council, a state agency.

See page 202 for a complete list of donors to BkMk Press.

Library of Congress Cataloging-in-Publication Data

Names: Lawson, Patricia, 1942- author.
Title: Odd ducks : stories / Patricia Lawson.
Description: Kansas City : BkMk Press, University of Missouri-Kansas City,
    [2020] | Summary: "These nine humorous stories, set in and around
    Kansas City, Kansas, from the 1950s to the early 21st century, often depict
    caring adults mentoring awkward but talented young people, whether in a
    community garden, a library, or in one-on-one advice. Other characters
    feel like outsiders in their own neighborhoods or become outsiders when
    visiting unfamiliar places in town"-- Provided by publisher.
Identifiers: LCCN 2020017486 | ISBN 9781943491230 (trade paperback)
Subjects: LCSH: Kansas City (Kan.)--Fiction.
Classification: LCC PS3612.A954236 A6 2020 | DDC 813/.6--dc23
LC record available at https://lccn.loc.gov/2020017486

ISBN: 978-1-943491-23-0

This book is set in MrsEaves and Galahad.

Contents

for Lester

Dead Duck

Next door lived a father who was much happier than Carol's father. Like her father, he was a poorly paid salesman—he had sold pop machines, kitchen-cabinet hardware, and TV antennas, among other things—and he kept having to change jobs because of problems at work, but none of this ever seemed to depress him but rather to make him buoyant, ebullient. He was a large man in his late forties with slick, dark hair, who, her parents said, was part Irish.

The family was jollier than her family. The children were fatter than Carol and her brother and sister, and when Carol was lucky enough to be invited to join the neighbors at supper, the family, whose name was Waters, had more food on the table. Following a quick Catholic prayer, the family ate joyfully and noisily. There was no parsimony, but a huge platter of garlic toast, perhaps a large casserole of macaroni and cheese, homemade and very yellow, not some pale imitation originating in a box.

Carol understood one of the reasons for Mr. Waters's happiness was the beer he always had at hand. Sometimes his temper would break loose, and he would turn red in the face and yell at his children, even pull off his belt and start swinging. But most of the time he was in fine fettle. He would hug his sons about the neck, kiss his wife on the cheek, tease his daughters. There were four pink-cheeked children, all very talkative, except the oldest girl, Mary Elizabeth, who was now dating and walked about thoughtful and remote.

The Waterses were all devout. In the girls' room was a small statue of the Virgin, to whom Mary Elizabeth and Dorothy, the younger daughter, offered devotions and prayed for forgiveness of their sins. Dorothy, Carol's friend, explained the difference between mortal sins, like killing someone, and venial sins, like lying.

"So if I say your outfit looks nice and it doesn't, it's a venial sin?" Carol asked.

"That's right."

"But if you say it's ugly, that's being mean. And isn't being mean a venial sin too?"

"Yes, but you shouldn't lie."

"Then you have to sin. You're trapped."

"If you can't be nice, don't say anything at all."

"What if the person asks?"

"Don't answer."

"But isn't that being mean?"

Carol and Dorothy had these little discussions all the time, or they talked politics. Truman's last year was ending, and Stevenson and Eisenhower were in the running, though Stevenson was not faring well, according to Carol's father, who adored Adlai. He had never known a presidential candidate so droll.

The Waterses were all pro-Eisenhower. "Ike's sure to win," Dorothy said. "Stevenson is dead in the water."

"Eisenhower's stupid. He doesn't know a thing about running a government."

"Yes he does. He's a general."

But the topic they kept returning to was sin. Was cheating on a test, mortal or venial? Venial if you just did it on impulse. What about having intercourse if you weren't married to the person? "Sister Catherine said if you act on impulse, it's venial; if you think about a sin, it's mortal," Dorothy said. "And she says everybody thinks about such a thing. You don't think about it when you smack your sister, but you think about *that*. So you should never, ever do it. Because, unless you're forgiven, you go to hell."

During these discussions Dorothy smiled and spoke with assurance while Carol listened in irritation, jealous because everything was so clear at the Waterses' house whereas at Carol's house, everything was either unstated or understated, accompanied by some glance or shrug.

Sometimes, when Carol's father had a drink in the kitchen after work, he could be happy, even silly; other times, he would keep quiet for long stretches, maybe eventually opening his mouth to make some running comment, usually sarcastic. "That child," he might say of someone in a TV commercial, "looks rather pie-faced."

The puzzling thing was that, according to her grandmother, Carol's father had at one time been a "hail fellow"—in his teens and twenties anyway. In high school he had been in a group that called themselves The Wiseacres. At dances they sat in the middle of the dance floor with crazy hats on. Her father had given a speech in front of his high school, demanding that teachers should feed bodies as well as minds and cook chicken and dumplings for all. He had once been suspended for bringing a goat to school.

But now he was a quiet, thinnish man, who stretched his head around to catch something on television, looking as if he could not possibly have heard correctly, it was so absurd. The local television newsman reported flash flooding "in the bottoms." "In the bottoms?" her father would say quietly, lifting his eyes upward. Everyone, even the youngest child,

Gerald, who was six, was expected to get the joke but not to comment. Sometimes he raised his eyebrows, like Groucho Marx, in mockery or disbelief, but usually outsiders missed the look because he did not exaggerate like Groucho, and his voice was so deadpan.

"Your father is a pessimist," Dorothy said. "He's a nice man, but he isn't optimistic like my father."

"He's very optimistic," Carol said, though she was, at the least, committing a venial sin saying so. Yet she knew the importance of optimism. And her father certainly *tried*. He had read Norman Vincent Peale and *How to Win Friends and Influence People*.

The trouble was he was not by nature talkative or active. He hated to be disturbed when he was reading. "Kindly remove yourself," he would say to some noisy child. Or he would withdraw upstairs. He could not tolerate noise, unlike Mr. Waters, who was like a fish out of water without some kind of family ruckus going on.

But sometimes he did something that seemed to indicate the "hail fellow" part of him was alive and well.

One hot, mid-August evening he drank several beers as he sat outside on the front porch. Carol was there too, reading *Photoplay*, and Gerald was reading comics as he lay on the porch swing, pushing it lazily with his foot. Carol watched him turn the page excitedly with one hand and scratch his pecker with the other. Lying at their feet on the porch, panting, was their neighbors' mongrel dog, Lucky. The collie part in Lucky had given him long hair.

"He's suffering," her father said, grinning out of the side of his mouth.

Carol's mother stood in the screen door sipping iced tea. "Who is?"

"Lucky. He's dying in this heat. I'm giving him a haircut."

"I hope you're not serious."

"I'm very serious. Bring me the scissors."

"Cliff, the neighbors will kill us."

"That dog has to be going nuts, I tell you." Lucky's ears twitched a little, and he half raised himself and bit at a flea. "He'll be much happier without all that hair."

Despite her mother's protests, Carol was told to go and find her mother's biggest pair of scissors. The dog lay still while Carol's father removed hair from below the belly and on the legs and tail. When the cut was finished and Lucky was standing again, everyone gasped because the haircut was so terrible. Big chunks of his coat had been taken out so irregularly it looked as if a child had gotten to him with a pair of grade-school scissors. The dog himself looked baffled and lay back down and bit at his tail.

Later Carol's mother called Lucky's owners to apologize, repeating several times how embarrassed she was. When she hung up, she said they had taken it pretty well. Carol's father shrugged his shoulders, stared at the clumps of dog hair lying about on the porch floor, and went inside to read. Her mother said, "I hope dog owners don't form a posse and come after your father."

But none of the neighbors said anything, choosing to ignore the matter as either unimportant or in bad taste. Except for Mr. Waters, who came next door to congratulate her father. "The damned dog's needed his hair trimmed all summer." He handed her dad a Hamm's and sat down on the front porch to talk about Ike. Carol watched and listened to them from inside as she lay on the sofa with a small fan positioned to blow across her body. She could see her father wince from time to time.

"You know I prefer Adlai, Francis," her father said softly, sipping the Hamm's, staring at his neighbor with worried eyes, then grinning. "He has a bit more hair."

Mr. Waters laughed and did a strange thing. He walked over to where her father was sitting and clapped him on the back. He put an arm around him and gave him a half hug. "*Frank*, Cliff, call me *Frank*. What the hell," he said. "I know you like the man. You've got your goddamn sign up. It takes all kinds in this country." Suddenly she liked Mr. Waters a little when she had never liked him much before.

Thus began a kind of friendship. Sometimes it seemed her father gloried in it. He had no other friends—he had long ago quit palling around with his former best friend, Lance Mitts, another former Wiseacre. Outside, talking to his neighbor as they drank beer, his voice grew louder to match Frank's voice. Walking beside Frank, Carol's father seemed to strut a little. But apart, he made disparaging comments. "He puts it away pretty fast," he said of his neighbor, whom he had dubbed the *auctioneer* for his volubility. "So many syllables, so little sense." He complained about his crudity. "He burps in syllables," he told them. "Pitches too." Yet he basked in this new friendship. He reminded them his buddy had suggested the two of them go duck hunting together in the fall. He was considering.

"Duck hunting! You'd be crazy," said her mother.

"I went hunting when I was a boy." Her father winked at both of them—or neither. Just being asked to go hunting had put him in a good mood. "When Lance and I were twelve, we killed several squirrels."

"What did you do with them?" Carol asked.

"Nothing. Squirrel meat leaves something to be desired."
He rolled his eyes upward.

"People do eat squirrel," said Carol's mother. "It's
terrible to kill something you won't eat."

"That's what boys do." He stuck out his chest a little.
Carol looked for the little lift of the eyebrows or his sideways
grimace but saw neither.

The hunting idea had come from Mr. Waters after he
had gotten pretty drunk one Saturday afternoon and begun
shooting pigeons with a pellet gun. He not only shot and
succeeded in killing pigeons at his house but had come next
door, bearing the usual Hamm's, to take aim at pigeons
nesting on Carol's roof.

Hearing the gun going off right outside their window
upset her mother. "Cliff, you've got to make him stop. He
could kill someone."

"All right, all right," her father said. He had been
working on a crossword puzzle, and Carol watched him write
ankh for twenty-three across. He put down his number-two
pencil and went outside. Carol stared at the spaces he had
left—a three-letter word for small boy, inf.; a five-letter
word for hard candy, Br.—until she heard her mother's
scream, followed by a shot. Her father was holding a pellet
gun, sipping a Hamm's, and aiming at a pigeon roosting in
front of an attic window. He pulled the trigger, fortunately
missing the window but also the pigeon, which fluttered up
in the air and flew next door to rest on the Waterses' roof.

"Stop it this instant, Clifford," her mother shrieked.
"You don't know where those bullets are going to wind up."

"Pellets, Lou," said Mr. Waters, "pellets."

"Frank's an expert," Carol's father said.

When her mother shooed Carol behind her, Mr. Waters
laughed a beery laugh. "Good try. Give it another, Cliff."

Her father glanced around timidly, pointed the gun at the pigeon, and shot again. A splat sounded as the pellet went into a shingle. This time the pigeon flew away and stayed.

"You got rid of the bastard!" said Mr. Waters.

"I did, Francis, I did." Her father's eyes were shining. This time *he* clapped Mr. Waters on the back.

"Frank. We need a Hamm's, Cliff. I'll be right back."

Mr. Waters went home and brought back three six-packs and a deck of cards. "Are you game for a little poker? Would you kindly put these in the refrigerator?" he said to Carol.

Her father looked a little worried about how long his buddy was going to stay, but he turned to Carol and said with a little smile that was half grin, half grimace, "And would you bring out the card table? This appears to be serious."

Supper that evening took place in the breakfast nook off the kitchen. "There's no use in fixing a regular meal," said her mother. "It's too hot, and he isn't going to come in anyway." Eventually she sent Carol out with roast beef sandwiches and potato chips to the men, who were getting drunker and laughing louder and louder. Carol heard the end of a dirty joke that asked the question, *How far is the Old Log Inn?*, and her father looked embarrassed and exclaimed several times about the sandwiches.

She looked over their shoulders. They were playing five-card stud, and her father held a pair of sixes and a pair of threes. Mr. Waters had three jacks. There were small piles of quarters on the table to each man's right, and Mr. Waters's pile was the larger. She would have clued her father in somehow about the three jacks, but he was looking out over the lawn, so she sat on the stone porch railing to eat a cookie and watch their neighbor closely to make sure he didn't cheat. Mr. Waters told several more stories and a joke about a dickless man. If he had a winning hand, he would slap his cards over on the table at the punch line. He told Pat-and-Mike jokes: "A parishioner tells Father Mike that Father Pat has only told him to say a few Hail Marys after the man confessed to sleeping with his neighbor's wife and isn't that terrible nice and easy of him. Father Mike says, 'Only Hail Marys! Why, Pat, the man committed a mortal sin. He told me he stuck it in her pussy every night for a week.' 'Well,' says Pat, 'The Hail Marys. And some catnip for the poor kitty.'" At "poor kitty" Mr. Waters slapped down a full house.

"My sincere apologies, sweetheart," Mr. Waters said to Carol after telling the last joke.

Her father didn't laugh this time. "It's getting late," he said to Carol. "Shouldn't you be going in?"

"Sorry, Clifford, I'll tone it down." And for a while he did, but he soon started in on the asshole at work.

Sometime after ten, Carol and her mother heard the men laughing again and Mrs. Waters haranguing her husband to get himself home. "It's late, and you have to drive us to Mass tomorrow."

"Let up on me for Chrissakes."

Her mother went to the door to say it was time to come in. Mr. Waters lifted one side of his large rump off the metal porch chair and farted loudly. "I don't think the mosquitoes will trouble us anymore," he said.

Her father's jaw dropped. "Oh my," he said in his mild way. The beer cans were spilling out of the trash can. "Clifford, it's late. It's time for bed. Come in now," her mother said. Her father slowly rose to his feet.

"Time for bed indeed! I wish my wife was as friendly," said Mr. Waters. He too stood up. Lucky let out a piercing yelp. "I stepped on him," he said. "I didn't see him lying there. I must have tromped on his leg."

"No harm done," said her father. "He'll limp around awhile and then lie back down. He thinks he's a rug." He seemed to have caught something from Mr. Waters.

"Tomorrow we'll get us some more goddamned pigeons." Mr. Waters's deep voice rolled through the doorway like a wave. "You're a hunter, Clifford. We're both hunters. We'll get those goddamned pigeons. And in October we're gonna get us some goddamned ducks."

"Right, Frank, right." When he went inside, he said with a kind of awe, "My buddy next door tells me we're definitely going hunting when it cools off."

And in late October they did, though Carol's mother nagged. "Why in heaven's name are you going? You hate hunting. Why don't you go fishing?"

Her father did like to fish. When the family made their summer trips to the Ozarks, he went off by himself while the children stayed in the vacation cottage or swam or waded in the clear-water stream. He would be gone for hours, not returning until late afternoon, when he might appear with a couple of middle-sized fish. He would clean them, and her mother would dutifully put them in the freezer until there were enough for a meal. Once Carol had begged to go with him, but her father was so quiet, he sat so long in one place gazing into the water, the day was so sticky, she grew irritated and bored.

She had read in one of her father's *Field & Stream* magazines that fishermen who preferred creeks and rivers to lakes were "a breed apart." "They prefer solitude," the article continued. "In a hidden nook they find a still, dark pool, or they stride into the rushing stream to cast their line. While the gregarious lake fishermen bob about in boats on the waters of some sunny lake, the river man knows deep inside that the wild, ever-changing river represents our lot in life."

She wondered how a man who felt this way would be able to put up with Mr. Waters for an entire weekend. She had walked out of Dorothy's house one day in the early fall when Mr. Waters started making fun of her family while claiming to love them all.

"I worship your father," he said. "But I worry about him, about all of you, you're such a pathetic, puny bunch. You could set the lot of you on a bale of straw. You're so dark, little girl, you'd think you were an Indian or a colored. It's your mother's French blood makes you so skinny and dusky. The French are related to the Africans—it's a known fact."

When Carol reported this conversation, her mother became irate. "You're not going," she told Carol's father. "He's an idiot. He'll shoot himself in the foot, and you'll have to walk ten miles for help. Or he'll shoot *you*."

"I'll be careful." Her father was trying on his new red hunting cap in the mirror and looking quizzically at himself. He caught sight of Carol watching and grinned. "I think I make a swell hunter."

On a Friday evening in late October, her father set a small suitcase by the front door. In a heap beside it was a duffle bag with a hunting jacket, which had been loaned by Mr. Waters, the red cap, and a sleeping bag her mother had borrowed from a Boy Scout in the neighborhood. Propped up in a remote corner of the porch because her mother would not allow it in the house was a 12-gauge shotgun.

Her father sat huddled in his old brown sweater sipping coffee with a little brandy for his nerves since Mr. Waters was driving.

"You aren't going if he comes over here drunk," her mother said.

"Oh, he'll be fine, Lou. He's driven that road many times."

"If he's been drinking, you make up some excuse. Surely you have that much sense."

When Mr. Waters pulled his Buick around by their front steps and tooted his horn, her mother went down the front steps with her father to check out their neighbor. Carol was carrying her father's suitcase. Apparently Mr. Waters was not drunk because her mother made no objections and gave her husband a quick goodbye kiss.

Mr. Waters's friend's hunting cabin was about a hundred miles away. They would stop on the road for their supper and get up early and hunt Saturday and Sunday mornings. They would have coffee and donuts each morning before setting out. For lunch they would eat sandwiches their wives had sent along. Saturday night they would eat out in a local restaurant.

"And drink gallons of beer," Carol's mother said to Mrs. Waters.

"Oh, don't worry so much, Lou. Frank takes it easy when he hunts. Else he doesn't want to get up as early as he needs to. Now he might take a nip of whiskey out in the field now and then to keep himself warm while he waits by the blind."

"Oh, Lord," said Carol's mother. "I wish you hadn't said that."

———◇———

Her father had said he would be back home around four or five Sunday afternoon. "Make space in the freezer for several enormous ducks," he said, raising his eyebrows like Groucho.

Her mother said, "I'll believe it when I see it."

Nevertheless, Saturday afternoon Carol found her mother rearranging the frozen food and removing a roast to make space.

By four in the afternoon on Sunday her mother began to relax. Either her husband was dead in some farmer's pasture or he wasn't. Probably he wasn't. They were due home any time now, and perhaps he would return triumphant, bearing game. Her mother said she hoped the duck would be processed and would come home de-feathered, beheaded, and de-footed, looking just like a chicken so she could treat it like a chicken.

When the men were not back by 6:30, her mother went next door to confer with Mrs. Waters. Carol went along, hoping they'd be invited for Sunday supper, but unfortunately the Waters had already eaten. The remains of pancakes and link sausages and a large, empty can of grapefruit were still on the counter.

"If they're not home by eight, I may call the highway patrol," her mother said.

"They'll be fine. Don't you worry," Mrs. Waters said. She and Dorothy were scraping the leftovers into newspaper. Her mother was looking skeptically at the wall plaques. She had once said Rose Marie Waters was about the toughest woman she knew, considering she had Mr. Waters for a husband and four children to deal with, so why on earth would she have plaques with phrases like "Oh, mother of mine" and "sweetly dimpled smile"?

They hung around the Waterses' kitchen chatting, her mother sipping coffee, and then went home to check on the younger children and fix a bite. By 7:00 her mother was pacing. Around 8:00 she was looking up the highway patrol number when Gerald hollered, "They're back." They went outside to watch the two men unload the car, and pretty soon her father trudged up their front steps, looking gray faced, lugging the suitcase, the duffle bag, the gun, and something long, white, and stiff, which turned out to be a partly frozen duck. From his silence in parting from his friend, Carol guessed the men had had a fight.

"You got one!" Gerald yelled. "Holy moly! Where's its feet?"

Her father sank into a chair. "Lou," he said, "I need some aspirin and a stiff drink."

"That's the skinniest duck I ever saw," Carol's mother said. "But you got one." She poured him a drink from the brandy bottle. He sat there sipping, looking down at his shoes. Maybe he was feeling sorry for the duck. Carol hoped the duck had been good and dead when they had de-footed it.

"He had to cut its feet off with an ax to get it into the cooler. I don't know why it's so skinny. I'm just so tired, I can't talk."

"How did it go with . . . you know?" her mother asked, nodding towards the Waterses' house. Her father groaned softly.

"Oh," he said, "you can't imagine."

"What did I tell you."

"I know." He sat quietly in his chair in the living room, drinking his brandy and doing a bit of the Sunday crossword. After Lisa and Gerald went off to bed, he began to talk a little. Apparently, Mr. Waters had not stopped gabbing and joking the entire weekend. And he had passed out goddamn I-like-Ike buttons everywhere they stopped.

"I never saw a man with so much energy. The only time he stopped talking was when we were at the duck blinds, but then he drank. He sat and sipped from a flask all Saturday. He had two along. I never saw the like."

"What are we going to do with this dreadful duck, Cliff?"

"I don't know, Lou." He looked tiredly at the duck as if it were some pitiful relative who had shown up at his door without having phoned.

"He got nine all told. One thing about him, he can shoot."

"Nine!" said her mother. Her father went back to his crossword. Carol tried to figure out some of the words with him, then went to do her homework in another room. From the kitchen she heard the clank of dishes being dried and put into the cupboard. Then she heard soft voices and another groan from her father. She put down her *Weekly Reader* and went back into the kitchen.

"What is it?" she said.

Her father shook his head, but her mother frowned and said, "She's almost a teenager, Cliff. She knows these things."

"What? Tell me!"

"He tried to fix your father up with a chippie."

"What's that?" But she already had an idea.

"A loose woman. A woman from the tavern. But you can't say a word about this, Carol," her mother said. "Do you promise? Not a word."

Carol nodded.

Her father said softly, "There were two women. He tried to get me to come along, and I wouldn't, so he went off with one for an hour. I had to wait in the tavern because he took the car keys. They had the juke box turned up so loud. I tell you, Lou . . ."

"You mean he went off and did you know what?" Carol said. "If he thought about it, it's a mortal sin!"

Her father shook his head wearily. "He left me with the cooler with all the ducks and said to guard it with my life. Then he left. There was nothing to do, nothing at all, just the loud music."

"That was terrible, Cliff. I can't believe it."

"I must have been crazy to go with him. I've never been
so exhausted. How he had the energy for . . ." He stopped
and stared at Carol. "He said I was a poor excuse."

"What a terrible thing to do to you," her mother said.

"He must have thought about it. He had to. That makes
it a mortal sin," Carol said. Neither parent paid her the
least attention.

Her father rubbed the top of his head. "But today he
was nicer. He gave me this duck since I didn't get one. Not
a one." He groaned and got up from his chair and went into
the kitchen, retrieving the duck. It was missing part of its
head. It had begun to unthaw, so that its footless legs swung
around a little as her father, holding it out from his body,
turned. "I missed every last one of them. I'm no good with
a shotgun. I'm ridiculous."

"Well, so what if you can't shoot. We have grocery stores.
Anyway, the one he gave you is pathetic," her mother said.
"We could just bury it in the backyard." She laughed a little.

Carol picked up on her mother's mood, hoping to cheer
her father. "I know what we can do. We could stuff it and
put it on the mantel. I know, I know!" She began to shriek.
"We could cross its legs and put shoes on it. We could put a
cap on its head to cover what's missing." She heard herself
laughing louder than she felt like laughing.

Her mother laughed too. "It's a pathetic duck. What we
should do is take your picture with it, Cliff. Stand up. Now,
hold it up. We'll put it on a Christmas card. People will get
a kick out of it. No, no, hold it out a bit. Higher."

Held off to the side by its neck, the skinny duck's body
seemed to elongate, as if it had suddenly untensed. It was
like the rubber chickens comedians used or the duck on *You
Bet Your Life* and somehow like a miniature version of her

skinny father, except that the duck's head was shattered, and her father had cocked his head to the side and was smiling out of the side of his mouth.

Her Religious Advisers

Carol and her mother and father headed down a green-carpeted corridor in the hospital to the room of Mary Gerardi. Carol had not really wanted to visit. Seeing someone so close to death scared her, but she felt, at eighteen, that she could handle it. And, as her mother said, "She always liked you so much, Carol."

Gerardi was Mary's maiden name. For a while she had been Mary Hockaday when she was married to Eddie Hockaday, who was Carol's father's cousin. But Mary and Eddie had separated because Eddie was a terrible alcoholic and had gotten mean-tempered at the end. As he was dying, Mary visited him, but right after his death she took her maiden name back. Carol's grandmother said Eddie, who was her nephew, was no good. When he was growing up, her sister had spoiled him rotten. Still, he'd made a mistake marrying Mary, who was for one thing, Italian; for another, Catholic; for a third, a drinker herself, so how could she help him; and for a fourth, not even a good Catholic. But Carol's mother liked her anyway.

Eight years ago, when Mary was both a new divorcée and a widow, she moved to Kansas City to take a job as a key punch operator. Since she was rather hard up, Carol's parents had hired her to babysit in spite of her being a big smoker. She had a smoker's cough, and she smoked until the glass ashtray was full, dumped it out, and smoked some more. If she got to laughing her husky laugh, she would cough until it seemed she would choke. Carol's parents fretted that she might fall asleep with a cigarette and burn the house down.

But Carol adored her because she told wonderful stories, both old-fashioned ones and little offhand stories that were sketches. Often the sketches took a real person and linked him or her to some fictional character. For instance, the woman who came to the door to sell magazine subscriptions used to be one of the wicked stepsisters in "Cinderella." Mary said, "No one ever married her because she wasn't much to look at and shrewish to boot. Eventually Cinderella kicked her out of the palace. Being married to a prince, she didn't have to be so nice. So now the poor stepsister's doing the best she can, and since she always was a talker, she went into sales."

The year Mary was dying, 1961, was the year Carol was in her first semester at college. Her freshman composition instructor was a former nun named Marcelline Rourke, who had given up her habit and apparently her chastity (she was married now) but not her love of rigor, which meant they were saddled with learning lots of grammar and examining their values.

Mrs. Rourke got right down to business. Their first composition was to be entitled: "An Exploration of My Religious Beliefs." Their teacher said she did not care what they were—they could be atheists or Holy Rollers—but she did expect an honest accounting because they were adults now and should know what they did or did not believe. Like

other students, Carol didn't know these things, or knew
them vaguely, though she might have been a bit more troubled
than some.

Her father had been raised in both the Baptist and
Methodist churches, but he never said a thing about religion;
her mother leaned toward Universalism. She was fond of
saying, "All the world religions can teach us something,"
but you could only build a vague essay around *that*, and Mrs.
Rourke detested vagueness. "When you think vaguely," she
told the class, "it's as if a swarm of fruit flies inhabits your
brain. Vagueness begets more vagueness. What you must do
is demarcate what you don't know but can *come* to know from
what you don't know that is unknowable."

Carol's essay was filled with I-don't-knows. She did not
know if God, heaven, or hell existed, but she liked to think
God and some sort of heaven did and hell didn't. She thought
everyone should be nice to people and, as far as possible,
animals. She thought it was useful to pray to someone you
could imagine, but if you didn't have available the picture
of "Jesus with the light brown hair," as her mother called
him, well then, why not picture St. Christopher or some
Old Testament figure?

She could not support any of those tenets with logical
proofs. All she had was anecdotal evidence, and, trying again
to please Marcelline Rourke, she labeled it as such. Thus,
the paper became more of a narrative and less of an argument,
and that was why, her teacher wrote at the bottom of the
page, she could not give Carol an *A*. "Furthermore, please
avoid dangling participles," she added in her tiny, neat
script. "Dangling participles are stylistic indicators of unclear
thought."

"I once believed in God and heaven and hell
unquestioningly," Carol's essay began. She then launched

into a time when her mother had, at her grandmother's urging, gotten a religious teacher to come to the house. Carol was around ten. This came about because at the dinner table one night her grandmother had quoted yet another biblical phrase, perhaps "whither thou goest," and Carol had made the mistake of asking, "Who said that?"

Her grandmother looked startled and said, "You don't know about Ruth?"

Not long after, Mrs. Whitmire appeared at the front door. She wore a navy dress under a long gray coat and had on heels that were not high enough to be glamorous. She was a tall woman with white hair and a serious face, though she beamed down at Carol, her sister, Lisa, and their little brother, Gerald, when she was introduced.

"What nice girls," she said in a clear soprano. "And you," she said to Carol, "you like to read I understand?"

Carol nodded happily, as if a saint had paid her a compliment.

"Mrs. Whitmire is here to tell you girls Bible stories," said Carol's mother and made a joke about their knowing next to nothing about the Bible. Their little brother, Gerald, was excused because he was "not of the age of reason," which was eight, Mrs. Whitmire said. Lisa *was* barely eight and did listen. Mrs. Whitmire skimmed lightly over Adam and Eve, because they were familiar territory, and proceeded directly to the story of Cain and Abel.

Her delivery was riveting. She got down on her knees and with scurrying hand motions constructed Cain's and Abel's altars. To demonstrate the gathering of "fruits of the field," she plucked imaginary things from the rug. She heaved herself off the floor and, standing on tiptoe, had Cain swoop down and stab Abel. Then she looked desperately over her shoulder and dropped her voice into a lower register when God thundered, *"Cain! Yes, you!"*

But her question and answer sessions were less compelling. Lisa began to twist her head to the side as far as she could. She played finger games. Finally she said she needed a drink of water and walked off. Carol was interested in the discussion, but Mrs. Whitmire's answers to her questions were unsatisfying. Why did God like it better for Abel to slaughter a poor animal than for Cain to give fruits of the field? *Well, because Abel was giving up something he loved.* But couldn't you love a plant? *No, you couldn't.* Why did Cain get so mad about God's preference for Abel? Why not just punch Cain in the nose? *Because Cain was filled with evil.* Carol should realize *how kind God was to Cain. Hadn't he spared him?* "And God gave him a mark and made him walk all over the world. And ever since, there have been two kinds of people, the righteous and the unrighteous," Mrs. Whitmire said.

Then Mrs. Whitmire pointed a finger at Carol and demanded, "Which are you?" Before Carol could answer, Mrs. Whitmire said, "Think about it carefully."

She bent towards Carol and said, "What is the greatest sin of all?"

Carol guessed the story held the clue to the answer and offered tentatively, "To kill someone?"

Mrs. Whitmire smiled kindly at Carol's naiveté. "No, my dear. The greatest sin is to kill yourself. Because God can forgive you if you kill another person, just as he forgave Cain, but he can't forgive you if you kill yourself."

This made a kind of sense, so Carol guessed it was true, but she didn't think it was fair.

Then the woman gathered her things to go, went into the kitchen, and thanked Carol's mother, who must have paid her five or ten dollars. As she was putting on her coat, she leaned towards Carol and said, "And next time, I'll tell you about Daniel in the lion's den."

As she was walking out, Carol's mother happened to look out the window and notice there was someone in Mrs. Whitmire's car.

"Is that your sister?"

"That's my daughter, Dora. She usually drives me. I don't drive any more."

"Wouldn't she like to come in next time?"

"We'll see. She's rather shy."

When she had gone, Carol told her mother Mrs. Whitmire had said suicide was the biggest sin in the world.

"I don't see how committing suicide would be worse than committing murder," her mother said.

"Because it's too late. God can't forgive you. And then you're in hell forever."

"God can't forgive you after you're dead?" Her mother frowned. "I thought she was just going to tell stories."

Their religious teacher only came three times. During her second and third visits her daughter, Dora, sat nearby, drank a cup of tea, and read religious magazines she had brought with her. She seemed pleasant, though she said little. She was shy, tall, with gray-framed glasses and hair only a little less gray than her mother's.

During the second visit Mrs. Whitmire fulfilled her promise to tell about Daniel's adventure with the lions. Mrs. Whitmire had a fairly realistic lion's growl, but Carol could see she had borrowed, maybe unconsciously, bits from the fairy tales, especially "The Three Billy Goats Gruff," because the lions were big, bigger, and biggest and were brothers. Daniel, in the scarlet cloak Mrs. Whitmire gave him, resembled Little Red Riding Hood, and the lions, a three-bodied troll or wolf. She could picture Daniel easily enough after Mrs. Whitmire's description of "tall, strong, muscular, and blue-eyed." He looked like a taller version of Paul Newman.

However, she had trouble imagining Shadrach, Meshach, and Abednego, the three men who had been thrown into the fiery furnace along with Daniel by the evil king, Nebuchadnezzar.

"What did they look like?" she asked her teacher.

"Oh, tall, strong, and brown-eyed."

"Triplets!" Lisa said.

Again, a discussion followed the stories. While Lisa squirmed, Mrs. Whitmire told them the message was there were good people and evil people in the times of the threesome, and the evil people got burned in the flames or devoured by lions, but God saved the good ones. When Carol pointed out that God had spared Cain, Mrs. Whitmire said, "Mysterious are the ways of the Lord." It was also puzzling why Daniel's enemies' children would have to be devoured too, but Carol supposed that was just another mystery. She could not fathom these mysteries then, nor could she now. But at least she was able to incorporate them into the composition for Mrs. Rourke in the section about things unknowable, along with victims of Nazi concentration camps and babies who died in earthquakes or on the Titanic.

When Mary babysat for them shortly after one of Mrs. Whitmire's visits, Carol asked her if she knew the story of Shadrach, Meshach, and Abednego. Mary said, "Barely," so Carol retold it for her and then asked, "What do you think they look like?"

"Let me have a cigarette, and I'll tell you in a minute."

Actually, it took three cigarettes and putting Lisa to bed and checking on Gerald before Mary continued. Then she fixed Carol a glass of Ovaltine and herself a whiskey and water and said, "Shadrach and Meshach looked a lot like Tweedledum and Tweedledee, though their dress was different. They wore paisley robes and wide, red cummerbunds, Shadrach and Meshach, I mean. You remember Tweedledum and Tweedledee, don't you?"

"Yes."

"Shadrach and Meshach were twins, a bit plump and not so handsome now that they were past forty and prematurely bald. One of them was very outgoing, Shadrach I believe, but Meshach was a shy fellow. Such a gentle soul. But unfortunately, he let his brother do all the talking, and that got them into trouble.

"Shadrach was very athletic. He could throw the javelin, and he would have killed the people who put them in the furnace if he had had a javelin handy, but he didn't. Another interesting thing about Shadrach is that he had very leathery skin from being outside so much, kind of the texture of beef jerky.

"Now, Abednego was a lot older—eighty or ninety, no, no, at least a hundred or two hundred. Now I remember. He was two hundred and forty. In spite of that, he was very flexible in his joints and could bend himself into knots. Anyway, there they were because the king's men had it in for them. I forgot the king's name."

"Nebuchadnezzar."

"That's right. They got into this fix because of Shadrach's boasting. He had too much confidence, if you ask me. The furnace didn't bother him. He could be out in the desert all day and not even get a trace of sunburn, but the other two were worried. Abednego's thinking was as twisty as his body, and he wondered if maybe they shouldn't just go along and pretend to worship the golden idol. Meshach thought it was artistic, though he was pretty sure it wasn't anything more than an interesting gold object. Did Mrs. Whitmire tell you what it looked like?"

"She just said it was big and gold."

"Then I think it looked like the Cheshire cat in *Alice* but with a body."

Carol laughed in disbelief.

"Anyway, they probably couldn't have talked their way out of it because the king's troops were so set on burning them up, and Shadrach wouldn't knuckle under. 'Who cares about your old fiery furnace,' he said. 'God will protect us.' In they went. Abednego told them to suck in their breaths as hard as they could and think themselves thin, and Shadrach said well, all right, but they didn't need to worry because they were in the right, and God would protect them, and Meshach thought, well, God might protect them or He might not, but maybe if He didn't the Cheshire-catlike thing would, so he did have a little hope, but a lot more despair. Well, as you know they were all saved, but he was burned the most, being fairer than Shadrach and fatter than Abednego. He came out a little bit pinker and hotter than he went in but otherwise none the worse for wear."

"But which one of them was right?"

"They were all right in one way or another."

"How did Daniel get the lions to leave him alone?"

"My guess is he had a prior connection with lions, kind of like Androcles," she said. "It pays to be nice to them."

Mrs. Whitmire, on the other hand, seemed to take everything straight from the Bible, except other things she might have taken from fairy tales—a stain made worse by scrubbing, talking shrubs, clothing that conferred invisibility.

She told them the story of David and Goliath and finishing Goliath off with a magic stone smack between the eyes that made him sway back and forth and then topple. She reenacted the scene, tilting dangerously right and left on her pumps, but did *not* fall to the ground but only leaned forward. She ended with: "And David remained right in the ways of the Lord for a good long time, and Goliath was consigned to the flames."

Carol thought she meant the flames in a furnace.

"Oh, no," said Mrs. Whitmire. "I mean the flames of hell. Let me read." And she opened her Bible to the back and read about being flung into a lake of fire. That done, she told about the beautiful alabaster gates of Heaven that opened for the blessed. Lisa was all ears.

Their mother seemed a little cool when she paid Mrs. Whitmire this time, and she said to Carol after the woman left, "I think she got a little lurid." Mrs. Whitmire had told the girls, "You who are of the age of reason must take care to be saved, for should you die unrepentant, your bodies will feel the flames."

"Don't worry," Carol's mother said. "She exaggerates."

But Lisa did worry. And when Mary was babysitting several days later, Lisa timidly told her she was scared of going to hell.

"Of course you aren't going to hell," said Mary. "Who said so?"

"Mrs. Whitmire, the Bible lady, said we could. If we're not careful."

"There isn't any such thing as hell," said Mary. "Believe me."

"Are you sure?" Lisa said. Carol waited for the assurance she knew was coming, which she loved hearing but could not altogether believe.

"Absolutely, positively—one hundred percent sure!"

"Oh good." Lisa relaxed instantly, but Carol knew adults would tell you anything. And Mrs. Whitmire had read the passage about the fiery lake right out of the Bible. It was all right there in Revelations.

In the corridor Carol's father stopped a nurse and asked timidly where Mary could be found and learned she had slipped into a coma. The nurse said, "That Mary's a character, isn't she! She'd lie there and make up stories about all of us. She told me I reminded her of the patient Griselda. I didn't know who that was so she told me the story, and then she said, 'But I guess you'd be Nurse Griselda, wouldn't you? I'm the patient.' I just adored her. I take it she didn't have immediate family?"

They were already talking about her in past tense. When they entered the room, Carol and her father hung back by the door though she could see the quiet, gray form in the bed. Her mother went up to Mary and took her hand. "Mary? Mary dear, can you hear me?" she said. They waited several minutes, and while they waited, they heard a husky laugh that almost made Carol jump out of her skin because she thought it was coming from the bed, but, no, it must be coming from the corridor. But when she stepped outside the room, there was no one there. After a little, they heard Mary's raspy breathing. Carol's mother sat for a long time holding Mary's hand. She said they might as well go on home; she just wanted to stay and sit with Mary a while. But less than an hour after they were home, her mother called and said Carol's dad might as well come get her because it was over.

⟨⟩

Not long after Mrs. Whitmire, Carol went through a religious phase that lasted three years. She joined her best friend's youth group, Servants of the King, and went on a number of retreats where they were told they were in their "golden days" and were lectured about the path to salvation. She read the Bible and reconfirmed that in spite of Mrs. Whitmire's having added certain touches, her Bible stories were essentially faithful to the originals. Mary was not to be believed when it came to religion. How could a Catholic, even a weak Catholic, not believe in hell? Carol quoted scripture so much her father finally told her two quotations a day would be plenty. Then at fourteen she lost interest and devoted herself to being popular.

Around this time, Mrs. Whitmire called Carol's mother, though they hadn't seen each other in several years. Carol answered the phone and recognized the voice on the other end, and for some reason, though she had been flattered by Mrs. Whitmire's attention when she was ten, she was now eager to get rid of her.

"How are you, dear?" came the high, sweet voice.

"I'm fine, Mrs. Whitmire. How are you?"

"Oh tolerable, tolerable. Are you still reading the Bible?"

"A little bit." Actually she hadn't picked it up in over a year.

"That's very good. Is your mother at home?"

From another room Carol listened in on her mother's conversation, which was mostly limited to brief responses, a lot of which were "I'm sorry to hear it." Something bad had obviously happened in Mrs. Whitmire's life, and apparently her religion had not protected her.

"Why don't you write her?" her mother said.

Her, it turned out, was Mrs. Whitmire's daughter, Dora, who was no longer communicating in any way with her mother. Apparently Mrs. Whitmire had strongly opposed her daughter's marrying a Jewish man. She would not give her blessing unless the man converted to Christianity, which he had refused to do.

"She probably said he was damned or some such," Carol's mother said. "I don't know, but Dora didn't marry him. But now Dora won't speak to her. She says she prays for her daughter's soul and misses her terribly. Dora's her only family except for a sister she never sees. She thinks God is testing her."

"Is she going to write her?"

"She has, but Dora won't answer. And if she calls, Dora says, 'I don't wish to talk' and hangs up."

Her mother sighed. "Actually, I think she called because she wants to come around for a visit and teach you girls more about the Bible. I don't know. Maybe she needs the money." Her mother looked at her carefully and smiled a little sardonic smile. "Would you like that? You wouldn't, would you?"

"No," said Carol.

They never saw Mrs. Whitmire again though she did call a few more times and plague Carol's mother with her problems, dropping religion almost entirely from the conversation except to say God was testing her. Then they lost touch. And then they read that a Miss Dora Whitmire, 55, had stepped in front of a bus and died of massive injuries. Carol's mother showed her the article in the newspaper, which contained a quotation from the driver about a woman stepping off the curbing "just so fast you couldn't believe it."

When Carol's mother called Mrs. Whitmire to offer her condolences, Mrs. Whitmire said it couldn't have been a suicide. Dora had always been absentminded.

"She won't believe it," said her mother. "I can't say I blame her."

"That would make Dora have to go to hell," said Carol.

"Oh," said her mother. "I guess it would mean that. But Mrs. Whitmire has a rather limited point of view, shall we say."

"I don't see why she didn't want Dora to marry someone Jewish. Everyone, like Daniel, she told us about was Jewish—I think."

"To Mrs. Whitmire you can't be Jewish *after* Jesus."

That meant that if Daniel, Shadrach, Meshach, and Abednego had been Jewish after Jesus, the lions or the furnace would have gotten them.

The year before Mary's death, when Carol was a senior in high school, she was a debater and a transcendentalist. Later, she became an agnostic, a compromise to please the college boy she was in love with and still dated, Calvin Amberson. Calvin had impressed her with his debate skills and atheism. He pointed out with delight how ironic it was that he, an atheist, would be named "unwittingly" for a religious leader. He outlined the various chronological inconsistencies in the Bible and made fun of the fact that Methuselah lived to be over nine hundred years old.

"Abednego lived to be two hundred and forty."

"Who?"

"Abednego." Then she realized Mary had made up that figure and felt a little silly explaining to this hard-edged boy, whom she wanted so much to impress, that the "fact" had come from her old babysitter. But when he seemed interested in this amusing detail from her childhood, she went on to relay Mary's descriptions of the biblical threesome.

"That's wonderful," he said. "According to her story, Meshach was an early doubter."

"I guess you're right."

"Yes," he said. "And if you think about it, the way she characterized them is brilliant. They represent ways of knowing. Abednego is a proto-pragmatist. Shadrach represents acceptance of a truth based on faith. I guess Meshach is also supposed to represent the ability to see things from various perspectives, a creative type. But she needed a spokesman for reasoning—someone like Descartes."

She had not learned about Descartes yet and thought he was referring to someone in the Old Testament, and that sent Calvin into hysterics.

"Well, there was an angel in the furnace. I thought maybe that's who you meant."

"No, no, God no!" Even then, when she had liked him more, she was annoyed by the way the right side of his upper lip curled up when he laughed.

"No, the angel would be another representative of faith. No, a serious omission. Oh well. It's still pretty good. Who did she say had it right? The pragmatist?"

"She said they were all right."

"Well, they can't all be right. They're mutually exclusive."

"So, I guess you can't believe in all of them?" It seemed to Carol that not to keep them all meant tossing out several babies in several bathwaters.

"At least you have to get rid of faith, my dear. There's nothing you can prove *that* way. At least you have to acknowledge *that*." He bent towards her, beaming before he kissed her.

All these "advisers" had thrown her religious life into confusion so that she could not defend a position for Mrs. Rourke. When she got the *B+* on her essay, she was disappointed because she had made *A*'s in English all the way through high school. She wanted to complain to her teacher about the grade. She *had* been as honest as she could about her religious beliefs, hadn't she? How could anyone really *know?* But it wasn't practical to oppose her teacher. Anyway, like Meshach, she could see her teacher's side. Mrs. Rourke had asked for an argument.

And then there was the dangling participle. Carol had written, "Picturing all the biblical characters, who became imprinted deeply in my mind, Mary's stories gave me delightful images." And they had (or Mary had), and because of Mary, Carol could picture people like Ruth ("she walked behind Naomi with her head down, but when she saw Boaz, her eyelashes touched her eyebrows"), and Noah ("he sloshed through water until his toes were pale-green prunes"), even Jezebel ("she wore thirteen gold bracelets on her right arm and thirteen silver ones on her left, which made her unlucky times two").

But she *knew* nothing, and, as Calvin often said of her, she was not a good reasoner. He was away debating when Mary died, and in a way, Carol was glad just to be with her family and not to have to deal with him. She was beginning to find his insistence on logical proofs tiresome. He had offered to help her rewrite her paper, if Mrs. Rourke would let her rewrite, saying he could provide her with a well-reasoned defense of atheism and had at his disposal some brilliant quotes from Bertrand Russell.

But after thinking it over, she said *no*. Borrowing his ideas would be cheating. Instead, perhaps she would approach Mrs. Rourke about rewriting the essay on a new topic. If her teacher would allow it, she would start off with the premise that nothing could be known for certain, but in this world we have glimpses.

"I'm going to use an exemplification to back up my argument," she would tell her teacher. She would take an outline and perhaps an introduction in to show her. "I had this babysitter once who told me stories," she might start out. "And all the things in her stories were true in a sense because they existed in my mind. You must rely on my personal testimony to believe they did exist. You have to take that much on faith."

Supposing you accept that they did exist, were they logically consistent? she would write. *Well maybe not always, but usually.* (She would use examples to develop the part about consistency.) *Did I learn something about life from them? Yes. You might call the thing I learned a* glimpse. *How can we know that the real world is any realer than the story world? We can only use our sense of having had real experiences. Again, you have to take on faith that I have not twisted my experience to fit the story or twisted the story to fit what I know about "reality".* (Calvin would like it that she put *reality* in quotes.) *How can we know that our understanding of the stories and the world is sound? Can we tell if there seems to be a match? What if our judgment is flawed? We can test it? How can we test it?* She had been up late jotting down all these questions. After two cups of strong coffee, they were coming to her one after another. It all gave her a headache, but she thought her teacher would be pleased.

She needed to make the appointment. "Where do I cut this off?" she would ask. "I don't want to write a book." But she would be more polite than that. After all, she did want an *A*. It would be a hard essay to write. It could go on and on. She had so many examples to pick from. Even Mrs. Whitmire, her old Bible teacher, could be in it. Mary had put her into a story once. She had made her into an ogress who prayed over people and ate them up with a celery stuffing.

But she was a comic ogress. Mary had her wail, "'I seem to have eaten a Christian by mistake. I thought all the people in the freezer were infidels. But what happened to the priest? It feels like there's a cross in my stomach.'"

And Carol had a concluding paragraph. "A world like that," she might say, "is almost like a world a religion makes up. What is the difference? Is there one?" She could even quote story after story from the Bible if need be. She would say that maybe the non-Bible stories weren't religion in the usual sense, but weren't they at least next door to religion? If not, she would ask her teacher, what *is* the difference? But she would be tactful.

"Right next door," she said out loud. In the way the laughter that was really coming from somewhere outside the room the night Mary died had seemed to be Mary's own laughter, and for a moment Carol had believed it was.

Butterfly Man

Fifteen kids from Polo's school, fourth or fifth graders just two weeks into their summer vacation, had been enrolled by their parents in the Young Urban Gardeners Project. Each child was given a trowel, garden gloves, and a T-shirt with an image of a pink peony and the phrase *I Love to Garden*. They got on the school bus every Wednesday around 7:45, groggy and longing for sleep or the comfort of the couch in front of the television, and arrived at the school around 8:20 where other kids were being let off. They reboarded again at 11:30 to be taken home for lunch.

They were given access to the garden and the school playground and to the restrooms and drinking fountains inside the school. They had the shade of a big tree they were told was a pin oak. They were also allotted: a sunflower seed to plant in a Dixie cup; sweet pea plants and a trellis kit; tomato and pepper plants and pots to put them in; small pots of rosemary, basil, mint, and lavender; a monarch caterpillar in a plastic cup with special food to help it change into a butterfly; individual ant farms; and a chance to take ownership of a worm bin for a day, though when one of the kids, Jesús Madrigal, took the plastic bin home and left it in the sun, steaming all but a few amazingly tough survivor worms, the lady in charge took ownership back.

She was a tall woman who wore earrings that were silver and turquoise. She also wore a name tag that said *Alicia*, knee-length jeans, a ball cap, and a sleeveless cotton T-shirt. Polo watched the way her arms flapped when she gestured. She liked to tilt her face to the sky when she talked. "Monarchs are the kings of butterflies," she told them. "When it comes to butterflies there is nothing more spectacular." She opened her hands and put her thumbs together, forming a butterfly, and wiggled her fingers to show how monarchs swooped toward their home in Mexico every year. She stared hard at the children and asked, "How many of you could travel several thousand miles without a map?"

"We don't need a map. We got *El Guepardo*," said a kid in a black and orange soccer shirt, referring to a bus that took people to and from Mexico. Some of the older kids laughed.

But the lady frowned because she didn't get the joke. Her short hair was a streaky, gray-brown, and when she sweat, Polo noticed her bangs stuck to her forehead in five separate strings. When she got excited, her face grew redder and more freckled, and when she was in the middle of a story that showed how gardening makes a difference, sometimes Polo thought she was kind of scary. She reminded him of the character Large Marge in *Pee-wee's Big Adventure*, who was a lady truck driver, who was really a ghost. He could imagine that, like Marge, this lady might be talking in a fairly normal voice, and all of a sudden her eyes would bug out, and her face would change shape, and she would reveal that she really was a ghost or, worse, a vampire. But he realized this was probably not the case.

—◇—

They were told they were apprentice gardeners. The lady in charge had told them that the first day. "How do we learn something?" she asked, not waiting for the answer. "We learn by doing. We become apprentices. Life," she said, giving them her fierce, angry look, "is full of apprenticeships. And gardening"—she stuck both her pointing fingers in the air—"is the noblest apprenticeship of all."

When they looked at her strangely, none of them ever having held a hoe before, she talked about the "contribution of plants" and why everyone needed green spaces, even in the city, and went from there to the rainforest. Polo had already learned about the rainforest in school, and the lady said almost exactly the same things. The rainforest helped the earth breathe. It was like a set of lungs.

Often while she talked, Polo thought about his rabbit. The rabbit was home all by itself in a hutch in the back yard under a tree, and Polo worried that a big dog would jump the fence, knock over the hutch, and kill the rabbit, Mr. Big Foot. Polo would rather be home keeping a lookout for dogs than hearing about the rainforest. But here he was. And today they were getting ready to plant a butterfly garden. He would rather make a garden for rabbits, but if he said so, the other kids would probably say he was weird or dumb.

"This is a butterfly bush," said the lady. She held up a weedy-looking plant in a black pot with a few flowers that looked like purple rattlesnake tails. While the kids sat at her feet on plastic cushions, she talked as she dug a hole with a shovel, sweat beading on her forehead. "We will watch it grow. And when the blooms open more, lo and behold, the butterflies will come and light!" She smiled the smile that meant they were supposed to nod and handed them other plants to put in the garden. The kids got off their cushions and onto their hands and knees to dig little holes with trowels while she called out the names: *sweet alyssum, verbena, lantana, purple coneflower*. When they finished, they went to sit at the portable tables and were given sheets of paper and crayons and told to draw something with a butterfly theme. "Think like an artist," the lady said.

Polo watched the kids he knew. Jesús made a simple butterfly out of triangles. Lucia Baeza drew a row of butterflies and colored their wings with rainbow colors. "Very pretty, Lucia," the lady said. Next, Lucia drew human heads on the butterflies. "My, my," said the lady. "Just look at that." Lucia was in Polo's class at school. She always got along well with teachers. He looked to see if she would color the heads different skin colors, the way she had done for two years. It didn't matter what she drew. It could be Aztecs or it could be robins, but the pictures always wound up with the multicolored heads. Usually the teacher put her pictures up and said something about the family of man. Polo was sick of those black, yellow, brown, and pink heads. He thought of drawing Mr. Big Foot with butterflies perched on both ears but maybe that would look silly, so he drew the tiger swallowtail butterfly because he liked the name.

The kid next to him, who had made the joke about *El Guepardo*, was named Miguel. Miguel had already gotten in trouble twice and received timeouts. During the timeouts he was removed from the rest of the kids and walked through the thick, knee-high grass they all walked through four times (twice each way) to use the restrooms and drinking fountains inside the school building. But Miguel was made to sit by himself on the fire-escape steps. He couldn't go above the third step, or the lady in charge would yell, "Third step—no higher!" Miguel said there were probably ticks in the high grass. Maybe poisonous snakes. "If I get tick fever or a snake bites me and I die, my uncles will sue. Martinez y Martinez. They get results."

Polo worried that Miguel might get in trouble again because he was not drawing with colors as they had been told to do, but with a black crayon. "I wish I had a motherfucking ink pen," he said under his breath as he worked on his drawing. "I can't draw with this shitty crayon."

"What are you drawing, man?" Polo asked. He could tell this kid was really an artist.

"He's a superhero. His name is Butterfly Man. That's what I'm drawing. You ever see *Spider-Man*?"

Miguel started muttering about how he hated the stupid Young Urban Gardeners and how he was going to pretend to be sick so he could stay home. "Young Urban Farters," he called them. He turned back to his drawing, making a sound like some kind of grinding machine starting up. "You gotta see that movie. It's awesome the way he can climb buildings. And there's this sticky crap that comes out of his body so he can make a net like a real spider. With the sticky crap, he can climb anywhere he wants. I don't know why we don't study motherfucking spiders instead of motherfucking butterflies, man."

Polo thought the kid was a little scary, but he seemed cool too. "What can Butterfly Man do?" he asked shyly.

"Aw shit, man. How do I know?" Miguel set the crayon down and stared at Butterfly Man. His wings were outlined in black, and inside the wings were big black splotches. In between the wings was a long narrow black body, and Miguel had drawn a v-necked shirt where a butterfly's chest would be. The lady in charge called it a thorax. Black tights covered the abdomen, and, at the bottom of the tights, clawlike feet stuck out. Butterfly Man had a mean look on his face. Out of his forehead grew two big antennae, and it looked like they were giving him a headache.

Miguel seemed stuck, so Polo tried to help him out. "Maybe he lays eggs where the bad guys are."

The kid gave him a look that asked *are you nuts, or what?*

"I mean," said Polo timidly, "like maybe the eggs have explosives in them, and later he sets an electronic timer, and he can blow things up whenever he wants. He blows up the bad guys."

"Yeah," said Miguel, whistling through his teeth. "Yeah."

The lady in charge was holding up Lucia's picture of the butterflies with the multicolored heads. "This is a beautiful vision," she said. "Look, everyone. Let's all give Lucia a big hand."

Polo clapped a little, but Miguel grinned and drew four heads like Lucia's at the bottom of the page. He drew broken lines from Butterfly Man's stomach. The lines ended in arrows. At the end of each arrow was a little egg about to fall on each of the four heads. "Boom!" he said under his breath. "Blooey! Blooey! Boom!" The lady in charge walked closer and looked at the picture. "Miguel," she said, "that's very interesting, but why is this butterfly dropping eggs on people."

"Because he's pissed," Miguel said, which earned him another timeout. The lady in charge said, "I'm sorry, Miguel, but I've told you repeatedly we won't have that kind of talk," and led him off to the fire-escape steps. She made him take along the water bottle each of them was issued at the start of the day and which they refilled inside the building after they had used the restrooms.

Miguel was already at the fifth or sixth step when the lady in charge hollered, "Third step—no higher!" Then he sat on the third step with his feet stuck out. Now and then he drank water, and one time when Polo looked at him, he was pouring it on his head.

—◦—

The second week the lady in charge introduced a lady named Poppy, who told them she was a griot, which meant she told stories. She was a short, round black lady, who wore a long denim skirt. Her hair was wrapped in a blue turban, and in her ears were huge gold hoop earrings, and on her arms, fourteen different colors of plastic bracelets. When she told a story, the kids sat in a circle on the seat cushions they had woven out of newspaper while Poppy stood in the middle and walked around the circle, stretching her arms out to the kids, pointing, wiggling her fingers with long red nails, or making wave-like motions with her arms. Sometimes she leaned over the kids, and the little ones scooted back to get away from her.

Polo wasn't crazy about having those long red nails close to his face either. The lady in charge told them Poppy was a *fantastic presenter*. She was really, really loud, but usually when she told a story, Polo's mind would wander home and to his back yard where Mr. Big Foot lived in his hutch. Or he would work his little toe in and out of the hole in his tennis shoe. Anyway, he'd already heard "The Grasshopper and the Ants" about a million times. And he didn't care much for Poppy's ending where the ants decided to share food with the foolish grasshopper and sang a little song she had written, "I'm Black, You're Green, but Let's Be Friends." And he was tired of hearing how cooperative ants were. She sang: "The things you do will turn out great. If you only learn *co-op-er-ate*."

Cooperating meant helping someone weed even if you were sweating all over. It also meant taking ownership and looking after things you had ownership of. Hearing this made Polo feel worse about Mr. Big Foot. Polo had ownership of him, but a dog could get over the fence at any time and take it away.

———◇———

Miguel was sitting on the fire escape again with his knees drawn up. This was because after the griot told them the grasshopper-and-ant story, Miguel said he had seen motherfucking ants swarm all over a dead grasshopper and carry it off. While Poppy read *Yertle the Turtle* and talked about democracy, Polo sneaked peeks at Miguel. The lady in charge had already yelled at him, "Third step, no higher!" and he came down from the step nearest the top. Later, when Polo looked, Miguel was sitting with his legs stretched straight out, but this time he had his heels together, toes pointed outward. He touched his toes together, moved them in, out, in, out.

Before they did their daily drawings, the lady in charge went to bring Miguel back to the group. She put a hand on his arm, but he shrugged her off. He lifted his legs high as they walked through the tall, itchy grass.

Later, Polo quietly got up and went to sit near him. "How's it goin', man?" they said to each other. Polo told him he'd missed *Yertle the Turtle*.

"I don't wanna hear no story about a motherfucking turtle. Tomorrow I'm gonna get sick so I can stay home and watch TV."

He muttered more and more softly, and eventually his picture took shape. It showed Butterfly Man with a girlfriend. She had the wings of a butterfly, but she had boobs and red lips and long black hair. Each had an arm (leg?) on the other's shoulder as they walked down a city street. The legs ended in claws. Miguel had written, *Butterfly Man Fell in Love with Butterfly Woman.*

Polo looked at his friend shyly. "Are they going to get married and have children?"

"Ten million motherfucking larvae," Miguel said.

The lady in charge was standing close by. "That will do," she said. "Miguel, I don't believe we can continue to put up with such inappropriate speech." And she took him aside.

Poppy, the griot, was telling the story of Br'er Rabbit and the Tar Baby, a story Polo's mother had already read to him. As usual, the children, except for Miguel, were seated in a circle, and the griot walked around, looming over them as she spoke. During the bus trip home yesterday, Miguel had said he was never coming back. Lucia said, "You can't anyway. You're kicked out."

Poppy had changed the story from the way his mother had read it. Instead of Br'er Rabbit getting mad at the Tar Baby and threatening to whop it upside the head, he went up to it to make friends but got stuck anyway.

Poppy leaned over Lucia's little sister, Graciela, and asked, "Have you ever seen a doggy come down the street and maybe you wanted to stick out your hand and pet it?"

Graciela didn't answer. She scooted closer to her sister.

"But you didn't pet it, did you, because your mommy told you it's dangerous to pet a dog you don't know? Isn't that so?"

Polo wondered what Miguel was doing right now and forgot the story until Br'er Fox came along and got the rabbit unstuck. Poppy talked about not looking before you leap and not straying from the safe path and sang a song about *being wary* and *sit-u-a-tions that turn out hairy.*

The lady in charge asked them what they thought of the story.

"Very educational," said Lucia.

Polo raised his hand. "I like the one better where the fox is going to eat the rabbit, and the rabbit gets away and hides in the briar patch."

The lady in charge put her hands on her hips and stared at him. "Polo, perhaps you need to be aware that there are different versions of the story. We shouldn't limit ourselves to a single interpretation. That is Poppy's own original version. She's pointing out a lesson, actually several lessons. And what did you learn?"

Lucia raised her hand and said, "Be careful with strangers."

"Excellent, Lucia. And tomorrow Poppy will tell you a brand new version of an Anansi story."

Polo was pissed.

But the next day Poppy wasn't there, and Polo was glad. Instead there was a lady named Kate, who was part Cherokee and whose ancestors had walked the Trail of Tears. Like her ancestors, she paid homage to creativity. She said each one of them had a divine spark of creativity, and she considered it her job to blow on the flame. "Today I'd like you all to make up a story about something you've learned. Write about an ant, a bee, a butterfly, or maybe a sunflower. I want all of you to become griots, just like Poppy. She's home today with sinus trouble. After we have our fruit punch and cookies, we'll share."

Polo was sorry Miguel was gone because he would have liked to hear a story about Butterfly Man, maybe one with his girlfriend in it. Next to him, Lucia was writing, "Once upon a time there were four friends. One was black. One was white. One was brown. One was yellow." He quit reading.

The lady in charge walked around and asked people how their stories were coming along. "I know you'll show Kate how creative you are."

Polo stared at the itchy patch of high grass and thought a moment. After a while some words and phrases came to him. He knew his story wasn't that great, so when his turn came, he read it softly and quickly, staring at the ground.

"Butterfly Man went out for a walk. He was walking and thinking. He had a friend who was a rabbit, and he went by the rabbit's house so they could go for a walk together and get some ice cream. There was a group of bad guys standing on a street corner making a drug deal. 'Hey Rabbit, how come you're in my territory,' said the main bad guy. 'I got a right to come in your neighborhood,' said the rabbit. 'It's a public street.'"

Glancing up, he saw he had the kids' attention. "'This is my street,' said the main bad guy. 'You're a prisoner. You're going to work for me for the rest of your life and clean my house and weed my garden and fix my car, and if you don't, I'll kill you.' 'No way,' said the rabbit. He started looking around for a place to run to. Then a bunch of other bad guys standing around pulled out knives and guns. They started to shoot the rabbit, but all of a sudden Butterfly Man flew over and made a funny sound—*zzzzzp*. And then he flew all around them and dropped butterfly eggs on their shoes. He dropped them on their heads and shoulders. Everywhere the eggs fell, they stuck. The eggs were inhabited by aliens that looked like little black caterpillars. The alien caterpillars climbed out of the eggs and grew and grew and began to eat up the bad guys. Then the bad guys screamed and yelled until they were all dead. Every last one."

Motherfucking had come to him too, but he had left it out.

After he finished his story, no one said much. Kate frowned at him and said, "My, my," and whispered to the lady in charge, who was shaking her head. "Why don't we move on to our next storyteller, Kate," she said.

When Polo sat back down next to Lucia, she shook her head just like the lady and said, "That's a really dumb story you told."

"No it isn't."

"Yes, it is."

She looked toward the school building. "You're going to be sitting on that fire escape. I bet tomorrow. Wait and see."

Adventures in Learning

They drove across a funny little wooden bridge. Beneath it, Elise saw a stream of yellowish water. She sighed several times, irritating her mother, which she didn't mind doing.

"Now, now," said Krista, "I don't want to see that droopy look. You'll spoil our adventure."

They were having another "adventure in learning," which meant boring and lame. Krista was forever searching for new horizons, some dumb retro store or art gallery or, like last week, a shop where a woman made hand-painted playing cards. They hardly ever went places Elise might actually enjoy like Schlitterbahn Waterpark or a store like Aéropostale.

Her mother had learned about this new place from a friend she'd made in tai chi. "Carlos says the woman is just amazing," she'd said. "He said she looks ten or fifteen years younger. He thinks it has to be the mineral water."

So they had driven to this old part of town, past empty buildings, past a rundown high school with a sports arena that had gotten weedy over the summer. Then they drove down this weird old crumbling road, crossed the little bridge, and now they turned off on a gravel road.

"Oh, my God. Look at all the trailers. It's a trailer park," said her mother. "Carlos never said . . ."

"Duh."

It was a really weird area—not city, but not quite country, and yet there were tons of trees, and then they saw a sign: *Crystalpure Mineral Water. Imbibed by Shawnee Over a Hundred Years Ago.* The place might have been nice once upon a time when the Shawnee lived there, but now it looked really lame and poor. Just not that much.

"You said they'd have a gift shop," said Elise.

"I thought there might be one. Be cool." Krista took a long sip of her iced latte. "Let's see what we turn up. Then we'll go get your Miley Cyrus CD."

"Can I get a hoodie at Aéropostale?" Elise's two best friends, Hillary and Mallory, had recently gone shopping without her because she was out "exploring" again with her mother, and they had gotten several lightweight hoodies. Elise had really cool friends, but Hillary and Mallory were absolutely the most amazing; plus, they had to-die-for names. It would have been really great if Elise had been named Ellery because then the three of them would sound even more like triplets, which was what kids called them at school. Ellery was the first name of an old mystery writer. Elise liked mysteries and had read all the new Nancy Drews, and maybe this summer she might borrow an Echo Falls book from Mallory's big sister, Candace. Candace said the Echo Falls books were a little dark but amazing.

Elise counted at least fifteen trailers, all located on little gravel driveways off the main drive. Some of them had tiny flower beds in front, and one or two had flowers planted in white tires, which looked dumb. All in all, it looked like a place hillbillies might live. That was a creepy thought. Hillbillies would pull out guns for no good reason. Kids at school said they had meth labs everywhere, so probably there were some in these very trailers. She repeated what she'd heard to her mother and said maybe they ought to keep the visit short in case one blew up.

Her mother only shook her head and pulled up to a big trailer the color of brown eggs, with a sign: *Crystalpure Office.* Nearby in the yard was a bigger sign with rusty red lettering that advertised mineral water at $2.95 a gallon. (*Buy four, get fifth* TOTALLY FREE, it said.)

"This doesn't look like a gift shop to me," said Elise.

The door opened, and a fat woman in a tight purple top and gray sweatpants stood in the doorway. She had white hair and a shiny face, and when she got closer, Elise saw purple eye shadow. There was a smell coming from her that was both sickeningly sweet, like some overpowering body lotion or talcum powder, and kind of smelly, like pee. The woman smiled through bright red lips. She looked really old, maybe seventy or more. If it was true what Carlos had told her mother about the woman looking ten or fifteen years younger, she could even be eighty-five.

Elise had figured out that what people thought was old varied a lot, age was a relative thing to people and that what her mother saw as young could really be pretty old, even older than someone like Amy Poehler. Hillary and Mallory and Elise had talked about this. They agreed there were three kinds of young: young young, which the triplets were coming to the end of; peak young, which was like Zac Efron and Miley Cyrus; and barely young, which would be someone like Anne Hathaway. Anne was peak young in *The Princess Diaries*, but in *Rachel Getting Married*, she was barely young, even close to being middle-aged, which was the part of life that was stretched out and boring.

To Krista you were middle-aged even in your sixties, but to Elise people that age were young old. The woman in the doorway looked peak old: not yet falling down old, but getting close.

And she smelled like a nursing home. She probably had on diapers. Elise had seen people in diapers when she'd visited her mother's great aunt Lois at Sylvan Manor. So how this woman could be amazing was beyond her.

"How did you come to hear about us?" the woman asked, and her mother did her goofy head-to-the-side look and started in about Carlos. "And I'm sorry, but he didn't give me your name," Krista said, and the woman said, "Mounty, Mrs. Betty Mounty, and yes, I know Carlos if he's the Carlos with the beautiful silver hair," and her mother said, "Yes, that Carlos. He said you were just a font of information."

"Oh, I so enjoyed talking history with him," said the woman. "I deeply enjoyed it. I bet you and your pretty daughter would enjoy hearing my little talk."

Elise wasn't about to listen to any little talk, which would probably be a long talk, but her mother would not like her to be rude and might take back the Miley CD offer and not even consider the hoodie, so she said, "Actually, I'd like to hear it, but I've been really kind of confined in the car, so I'd like to just stretch my legs, but you go ahead, Mom." Before they could stop her, she headed down a dirt road, looking around to make sure there was no smoke or weird smell, like from a meth lab. "I'll just take a little walk," she called back. "It'll be an adventure." What could her mother, who probably thought of herself as being like that Indian woman who made friends with Lewis and Clark and whose name Elise couldn't pronounce, but it started with an *S*, what could she honestly say?

"Don't go far," Krista said. "Keep to the main road."

"Duh."

"Oh, she'll be fine," said Mrs. Mounty.

Actually, once she got away from them and headed down the main drive under some big trees with leaves like hearts and saw how the path went down and down into deeper woods where a creek might run at the bottom of the hill, she thought maybe there would be an adventure after all. What if she saw a hillbilly? Would he (or she?) have a knife?

In front of a robin's-egg-blue trailer, a round-faced girl with long, fine hair sat on a metal step reading a Junie B. Jones book. There was no adult anywhere in sight though the girl looked younger than Elise by a year or so, which would make her either nine or ten. Elise had read those books when she was eight, so maybe the girl was slow.

The girl had protruding eyes, sort of like an angel fish. She stared at Elise's outfit. Today wasn't that special because Elise was only with her mother, but since they planned to eat out, she had worn her new metallic yellow cami with lace around the bottom, her black cropped pants, and pulled them together with flip-flops that had big black, yellow, and white flowers between the big and second toe. Mallory said Candace said you didn't always have to coordinate everything, but Elise still thought coordination was really important unless you totally knew what you were doing when you broke the rules, and Hillary and Mallory agreed.

This girl was not at all coordinated; her look was just trashy. She had on a faded, too-big, orange T-shirt that looked like a brother's hand-me-down and some old denim cutoffs, and you could tell those things on her feet weren't real Crocs.

"You want to go see a myna bird," said the girl in a kind of bored tone, as if she was used to introducing people to myna birds.

"I guess."

"Well, come on."

"I took a class on birds last summer," said Elise. "The Glory of Birds. We learned about all kinds of birds and genuses and species and things. It was kind of cool and kind of boring too."

"I like dogs better," said the girl. "Have you got a dog?"

"I've got a Welsh terrier, a bitch named *Lilybelle*." Elise waited to see if the girl would be shocked by *bitch*, and her eyes did open a bit wider, which proved she wasn't that informed.

"*Bitch* is what you call a female dog," said Elise.

"It means *whore*. What's your name?"

"*Elise*"

"Mine's *Amanda*."

Elise was surprised because she'd expected a low-class name, maybe *Emerald* or something. A girl at her school, whose mother had won a lot of money on a scratch-off ticket, was named *Emerald*, and she was pretty trashy.

"It depends on the context what the word means," Elise said. "We learned about context in my language-awareness class." Amanda stuck out her lip and looked confused. "It's like the total situation you find a word in. Like packaging," Elise added, trying to remember her teacher's actual words. "So when you're talking about female dogs, you're supposed to call them *bitches*. Haven't you ever watched a dog show?"

Amanda ignored the question. "I had a dog once, but she got run over by that brown pickup over there, and I'm sure as hell not going to call her a bitch."

Some people were hopeless. Amanda pointed to a green trailer with white shutters and said, "That's where the myna bird lives. Its owner used to be a professor."

"Yeah, right."

"You don't believe me?"

"I don't want to offend or anything, but why would a professor live here? My mother has a friend who's a professor, and he lives in . . ." Elise had almost said "a nice house" but thought better of it. "He lives near a college," she said.

Amanda knocked on the door, and Elise heard something squawking, " 'Ello there. Come on in." The man opening the door looked like the man that played the bald security guard in *The Princess Diaries*, Hector something, except this guy was not very healthy looking. He was wearing a rumpled Hawaiian shirt, and Elise wondered if he might be trying for a tropical look with the myna bird and all.

"Can you get Franklin to say more stuff?" Amanda asked him. The man brought the cage to the door. Inside was a black bird with an orange beak and yellow bands on its head. "Say hello to the young ladies, Franklin," he said.

The bird hopped around and whistled several times before saying, " 'Ello, 'ello."

"Tell them what kind of bird you are."

"Bad bird, woo-hoo. Bad bird." Elise thought the bird's act needed punching up.

"Where's your mother today, Amanda?"

Amanda looked down at her imitation Crocs and said, "I think maybe Sam's Club."

"And how about you, young lady? Were you just in the neighborhood and decided to stop in?"

Elise caught something sarcastic in the man's tone but she had nothing to fear. Her mother had much more impressive friends, including one who used to live in LA and had been a yoga coach for VIPs including a good friend of Gwyneth Paltrow.

"My mother came here to buy water," she said. "Mrs. Mounty is telling her about the Shawnee or something."

The man was drinking beer in a paper cup, and when he laughed, the beer sloshed over the top onto the floor, but he didn't wipe it up. There were stacks of old books and magazines and papers all around the living room. "Betty and her history lessons. They're about as valuable as that water she pushes."

"What's wrong with it?" Elise said.

"You might as well turn on your own tap, sweetheart."

"Come on," said Amanda. "I'll show you the river."

"Don't fall in," said the man. "Amanda, tell your mother I'd like her to drop by Saturday, in the afternoon if she would."

"Okay."

When they were outside, Elise asked if Amanda's mother was a cleaning lady.

"Kind of. She does other things too."

"Like what?"

"Oh, different stuff."

The conversation seemed to make Amanda depressed. Elise had the feeling her mother was probably a single mom like Krista but without the alimony and tried to think what Hillary or Mallory would say in this situation. They weren't all that nice to Emerald, but that was because she was so annoying. But if someone was really in need, they were nice. All three girls had been part of a club that raised money for a poor family by having their own garage sale. They'd actually raised two hundred dollars, mostly by selling their old clothes, including Mallory's leather bomber jacket, which had gotten her grounded though the jacket wasn't that cool any more.

"Hang in there," she said after a while.

"What?" Amanda's lip stuck out awful. Some day she might need plastic surgery.

"I kind of think," said Elise, "that some days are really hideous. I mean my mom's divorced, and I don't get to see my dad that much, so I know how you feel. I mean I'm guessing you might be like kind of in the same boat. You're a little young now, but you're going to find out some days are good, and others are the pits, and you just have to hang in there"

"I guess." Amanda shrugged.

Elise heard her name being called. Her mother was coming down the road toward her, carrying two jugs of mineral water. When she saw Elise and Amanda, she smiled, turned back to the car, and set the jugs down.

"Hey, lady," Amanda yelled, "you'd better lock up that water. There's a woman who steals it for her roses."

Krista smiled her goofy smile. "Elise, why don't you and your friend come hear about the Shawnee? It's fascinating material."

"I want to go see the river," said Elise.

"Promise me you won't get close to the edge."

"I'm not stupid."

"We'll be real careful, ma'am," said Amanda.

Krista went back inside the office. Amanda said, "That old bitch likes to talk about the Shawnee Prophet. He was the brother of Tecumseh, and they fought off the white man. She says the Prophet used to come to that old dried-up well of hers and drink, but how does she know that? She makes it all up like she does about the water. She just buys it at the store and slaps on her labels. Come on, the river's this way."

They passed a trailer where a woman in a red tank top was rocking a blond toddler. They passed a clump of irises where the blooms had fallen off. The path went downhill more steeply, and both girls stumbled now and then. Elise had to stop to pick stones out of her flip-flops.

The drive came to an end, and soon they could no longer see the trailers and were in a deep, green wood. Ahead Elise heard the water, sort of a chuckling sound.

It was like being in a fairy tale, like they were Hansel and Gretel, kind of. She wished Hillary and Mallory could have come. They liked spooky places and rivers and things. Behind Mallory's house was a little creek, and at the end of summer, Mallory's dad would dump a bunch of dechlorinator into the swimming pool and drain the water out through a pipe that emptied into the creek. He and Mrs. Nowak would supervise while the girls played around in their very own river. The water from the pool would make the creek water sparkling clear for just a little while, and the creek would rise and fill a little hollow carved into the creek bank. Then it would all disappear downstream. But for a short time it was as if the triplets, and sometimes Candace, had their own natural pool. They had named the pool *El-Ma-Hi*, which came from the first two letters of each of their names and sounded Indian or something.

"Better hurry," said Elise, "or I won't get to see it. My mother will come looking for me."

Amanda gave her a serious look. "My mother's abusive," she said. "I got a whippin' over nothing. But I bit her once to teach her."

"You shouldn't bite," said Elise. "But you could report her. She could get counseling and maybe get conflict resolution. My mom and dad tried it before the divorce. Well, honestly, it didn't work that great, but it might for your mother."

"Maybe I will turn her in," said Amanda. "I really miss my grandma. She died a month ago. She was a whole lot nicer."

Elise walked cautiously in case there were snakes lurking in the vines they were pushing through. Something tickled one of her toes, and she freaked, but it was only a roly poly.

When she finally saw the water, she was disappointed. It wasn't very pretty; in fact, it was a dark muddy brown, and in places looked almost black. What would make a creek or river (she wasn't sure which it was, kind of in between) so dark?

Right in front of her it ran slowly, but downstream a little it grew shallow and ran over rocks, and that was where that chuckling sound came from. The shallow part with the rocks was in the light, and there it looked kind of slick and yellowish. She thought of the story her own grandmother used to read to her, "The Elephant's Child." The little elephant was always getting spanked for his curiosity. When Elise had said, "That's abusive," her grandmother had laughed. The elephant's child was curious about what the crocodile ate for dinner and asked the Kolokolo bird, who said, " 'Go to the great grey-green, greasy Limpopo River, all set about with fever-trees, and find out.' " And what he found out was that he himself was supposed to be dinner. And that was what this river made her think of though it was more brown than gray.

They took a few steps closer to the edge of the bank. Amanda sat down near a little bush and reached around, prying rocks lose from the dirt to throw into the water. Elise did the same but did not sit down because she was afraid of poison ivy and snakes, and she did not want to get her new cropped pants dirty. Amanda was just wearing those old denim cutoffs, so she hadn't even thought about it. Obviously.

Elise wanted to give her a little fashion advice. What would Hillary and Mallory say to a girl with protruding eyes who was not at all pretty? How could you bring out her best attributes? Elise was thinking maybe she would just recommend that Amanda talk to her mother about starting off with some fashion essentials, some decent jeans or jean shorts, and maybe they could go to Old Navy, which wasn't that expensive, when she saw Amanda was crying. Big tears ran down her cheeks like the tears you saw in cartoons.

At first Elise thought Amanda must be jealous of her outfit and maybe a little sad because she was poor. So she sat down beside her and tried to give her a girlfriend hug, the way she always hugged her friends when they met before school. But Amanda just kept crying. Her nose was running, and neither of them even had a Kleenex. "I miss her so much," she said and sniffled a little, so now Elise understood and tried to think what to say.

She hugged Amanda harder. "Things will get better soon," she said, which was the first thing that came to mind. "Crying is good for you actually. It's therapeutic. We all need to vent sometimes, so go ahead and cry. I know if I lost one of my grandmas, I'd cry too. Not so much if the other one died." She sat there, trying to think what else to say. What would Candace say? She wished she could remember what her teacher had said when Rachel Newcomb cried in class because her favorite cousin died in a car wreck.

"Hang in there," she said again. But she felt totally weird and totally lame.

The dark river ran below them past the point where the chuckling sound came from and on out of sight.

Biker

Inside his apartment Stephen watched Sandra trying to pry open a stuck thermos lid with a table knife, which would probably end in her shattering the thermos's glass lining. He felt a familiar bur of irritation, but for a moment let himself enjoy its prickle.

It really was time to break up. Once there had been a slight upward momentum to the relationship, which *she* had goaded into existence, but now things were terrible. He had never liked her pale skin for one thing or her nearly invisible eyelashes. His skin, it must be admitted, was also somewhat pale and no doubt was one reason for his having been classified as a nerd in high school and college, but in her company he felt nerdier. Another thing he disliked was the false intensity with which she "studied" things—a pin-oak leaf, for instance, or an oddly spotted ladybug—to show off her pretended interest in "the world around us."

She could be relentless. They needed toe clips for their bikes, she insisted, and when he said "no rattraps for me, thanks," she inclined her head to the side, like a puzzled dog (an expression he recognized as totally fake because she never puzzled over anything) and explained how clips improved pedaling efficiency. "If you want something that catches on the terrain, go for it," he said, "but count me out."

He also disliked her car, an old VW Beetle, disliked everything about it and thought it all reflected her—the porelike perforations in the upholstery; the exterior color, a beigey pink, which resembled the tone of her skin when she was just starting to burn; the stupid cartoon about a VW she had taped to her glove compartment (a man staring at a VW lot and saying "Where's the Raid?") about which he had said, "not funny"; most of all the reeking car deodorizer in the shape of a butterfly.

And why, for God's sake, had she wanted to spend their Sunday pedaling fifteen miles into the "country" with a picnic lunch *he* would have to tote on *his* back. "It isn't even country fifteen miles from here. It's suburbia," he'd said. He saw enough of the suburbs when he stayed with his parents, more or less to keep them company, though he lived in town during the week in his tiny apartment while he finished his PhD.

As an alternative, he proposed biking to the Plaza and going to Barnes & Noble, maybe having coffee there.

"I can pack iced coffee in the thermos. Look! I got it open."

"No," he had said loudly. You had to practically hit her over the head. "I don't want a *suburban* experience. I want an *urban* one. I *want* to go to the bookstore." He noted that he often sounded petulant and childlike arguing with her, but that was how it had to be.

And so, wearing his yellow jersey and new lycra/nylon padded shorts, he led the way through the streets he considered safest for bicyclists, though none were *that* safe. Kansas City drivers were mostly inconsiderate of bike riders. Sometimes he despaired of ever being able to live the life he wanted in a town where biking to a shopping area was a major undertaking.

Still, it was nice at Barnes & Noble, at least for a while, even though it meant having to lug his helmet around inside the store. He left Sandra in the magazine section while he went to look at the store's meager collection on the hard sciences, leafing through a few books on reptiles before selecting one with sensational pictures of Gila monsters and hooded cobras so he could wow his upcoming summer zoology class. Today's students were visual creatures, and you had to play to their interests.

They drank their iced lattes and then glasses of water as they ate the egg-salad sandwiches she had sneaked in inside a tote bag. "It would have been nicer to have a picnic," she said. "Anyway, he's watching us"—she nodded towards the pug-faced kid behind the counter.

"He doesn't care," he said. "Why should he? Look there." He pointed. A homeless man was dozing at a table in a corner, a tattered gray bag on the floor beside him.

"Okay, but if the manager were here, he'd ask us to leave."

"No he wouldn't. People today don't make waves."

She set her jaw and went back to the toe clips. He really should buy them. "You're not getting full use of your upstroke," she said.

Again he explained his thoughts about overcomplicating a piece of machinery and almost slipped in, "I think we need some time apart," but she was bending over to pick up a dropped napkin, revealing bluish-white skin at the top of her forehead. When she was upright again, she said, as if she had heard nothing, "At least you should give them a try."

She took forever repacking the silly fuchsia Tupperware containers into her tote, and he was so annoyed that on their way out he forgot he was carrying the reptile book, walked past the alarm system without having paid, set off a buzzer, and had to explain to a frowning security man, who responded to his explanation with "Whatever."

"You need a good nap," she said. "You're really grouchy."

"I've got work to do."

"People's natural rhythms are low after lunch. People who are able to get into deep sleep, even for a few minutes, improve their mental efficiency."

He gave her his thoughts about the quality of research you were likely to come across in *Psychology Today*. She was silent only a moment. "A nap improves your disposition too."

When he got back on his bike, he noticed irritation was making him pedal faster. Even so, several blocks later, he was surprised to see how far ahead he was. Halfway up a steep hill, he glanced over his shoulder and saw to his delight that Sandra was at the foot of the hill, having trouble with her goddamn toe clips. It served her right. He pedaled to the top, enjoying the sense of strength in his calf and thigh muscles. He was in astonishingly good shape.

At the crest, he looked back again and saw she was still struggling. He supposed he should go back and help but didn't think he could stand to. There was sure to be a quarrel. He looked ahead at a long level stretch where the street was dark and shaded.

He considered for about two seconds. And he took off.

Immediately he felt an enormous thrill course through his body, equal components of fear and joy. She was out of his vision now, but she would eventually get going and come after him. Quickly he turned into the university campus where he taught and formed a plan. He would not go back to the apartment. Neither would he go to his parents' house because that would be the next place she would look. Instead he would double back and bike to another part of town altogether and just sit, and, well, examine things.

Did he have the courage?

"Yes," he said aloud. "I believe I do."

He took a crazy, zigzag path through the campus, down little streets, around buildings, through parking lots. Eventually he could see the same corner where he had left her, but she was gone, no doubt doggedly following their usual route to the apartment.

After peering about, he waited by the side of a limestone building, deep in the shade of a large gingko, plotting. Suppose he were to hang out a while in a part of town she was totally unfamiliar with. The area that popped into his head was the West Side bottoms. He might even cross the state line and find a nice bar where he could drink cerveza until it grew dark, maybe find a place to rent a room for the night. That would show her. He had driven along the border of the area countless times. Glancing west, you saw a neighborhood of small and medium-sized houses close together, partially hidden by a concrete barricade. Somewhere behind all that there was sure to be a nice little bar.

He decided to circumvent the Plaza to the west. Then he would head north until he found the right place. He would know it when he found it. It would mean a lot of biking, but he was up to it, unless he got a muscle cramp, which could make your calf muscle tighten as if it had been sculpted out of granite.

It was crazy, but he would do it.

He checked his watch. It was now about a quarter to four, and the day had heated up. It was a typical steamy Kansas City afternoon in late May, the wind out of the southeast, in the mid-eighties. Maybe twenty minutes or so of heat, unpleasantness, sweat, exertion, and risk before he could reach his objective.

He passed a country club where people were out sweating in the sunlight. To his left a man in a beige knit shirt and olive-drab Bermuda shorts swung his club, trying to drive a ball out of a sand trap. To his right four teenagers were playing doubles at a tennis court. One of the girls, who looked a lot like Sandra, seemed to be watching him.

He kept glancing over his shoulder but saw no Volkswagens, thank God. There was something menacing, almost predatory about them—perhaps because of their resemblance to beetles or their history as Hitler's people's car.

He pedaled past an area he might have chosen to live in if he could have afforded it. The houses were nice but not ostentatious, and the trees, good-sized. The area reminded him of his parents' neighborhood. In fact, that gray-blue frame house he was now passing was a lot like their house. Maybe it too had matching cream-colored recliners and Hummel figurines on the whatnot shelf.

He passed an aluminum company and a white stucco church. How odd to find the two in such proximity. What did it indicate about these people? He was headed downhill now, so it was smooth sailing for a little. Above him and to his right was the meager Kansas City skyline, its dozen or so tallish buildings hazy in the distance, as if separated by a thin curtain of grayish-pink gauze. Once in the area he was headed for, he would steer clear of the main streets and see what he could find on a side street.

But after pedaling up and down the steep hills, he found nothing, and he kept circling a looming billboard that advertised Volkswagens. "*Nada. Nada y pues nada,*" he said to himself, echoing some story he had once read. No little bar. Nada.

The streets had been fairly shady, but now the shade gave way to bright sun. Ahead he saw viaducts leading him westward. The gleaming whiteness of the buildings and streets made his eyes hurt, but he pushed on, his tongue and lips dry. He crossed the state line into a totally foreign area, the other Kansas City. Ahead he saw a flat street with light industrial buildings, but a bright orange cinder-block structure caught his eye. A restaurant and, yes, *cerveza* in bold turquoise letters outlined in black on the window. What luck! There was a parking lot mostly hidden by the building. He wheeled in and cabled his bike in a secluded spot behind the back door.

When he entered, everyone in the bar stared at him, almost as if they had been awaiting his arrival. They must have been watching him on the closed-circuit TV above the huge jukebox. No doubt they were wondering what an Anglo guy in skin-tight black shorts, backpack, and helmet was doing, fastening his bike to the chain link fence.

The bar was full of men, most of whom looked Hispanic to him, drinking beer and eating. Everyone was wearing jeans, and most wore T-shirts. A few looked dirty, as if they had just come from doing some sort of physical work. And it was Sunday! There were only a few women, three of them sitting together at one table, one very beautiful, wearing large silver earrings and talking animatedly in Spanish. She smiled at his bare legs and shorts and made some comment in Spanish. He caught *pálido*. He set his backpack and helmet on a table.

"What can I get for you?" said the waiter, a heavyset, fatherly-looking man.

"A Corona Light," he said.

"No Light, amigo."

"Corona then."

A soccer game was playing on another television set, located on a platform above the front window, and the men craned their necks to watch. He heard the popular sportscaster, whoever he was, shout *g-o-o-o-o-o-o-o-al*. It seemed Argentina was playing. The other team seemed to be English, or possibly Irish. Argentina must have scored because the people in the restaurant began whistling and shouting.

When the waiter brought his beer, he asked for water as well.

"Working hard?" the waiter asked him. "You look hot. Your face is very red."

"I biked here."

"No kidding. From where?"

"The Plaza."

"You're kidding, man. That's a long way."

"Well," Stephen said, "it wasn't so bad. I'm used to it."

The man smiled and walked off, stopping to chat at a table loaded with beer bottles where four men sat.

Watching other people eat, Stephen began to feel famished. The trouble was his book purchase had left him with only five dollars, which would barely pay for the beer and a small tip. He dug into his money belt hoping to find a little change. If he could scrape enough together, he might buy a side order of beans or rice. He studied the men in the bar, some of whom were relying on friends to buy them beer, and realized this must be how it would be if you were hard up. He got up to use the restroom and, glancing into the kitchen, saw the cook was watching the game on a small TV while he fried eggs. "*Huevos*," Stephen muttered, pleased that a bit of the Spanish he had taken as an undergrad was coming back to him.

On his return trip he was horrified to see on the closed-circuit television that a grainy Volkswagen was pulling into the parking lot.

My God! He went to the back window, lifting one of the greasy louvers in the blinds, and looked out. Thank God it wasn't Sandra's car but a bright yellow VW with flowers painted on it, using the restaurant parking lot to turn around in.

When he got back to his table, there was another Corona sitting there. He looked around to find out whom to thank for it, and a slim young man about his age in a red T-shirt with a large tattoo on his arm, seated at the table with three other men, nodded his way.

The waiter leaned over his table sympathetically. "Are you okay? Your face went bad for a moment. You looked like you saw a ghost."

"I thought it was my . . . this woman I know. She might be following me. I hope not." Stephen looked down, a little ashamed, knowing the man would think him foolish.

"A stalker? A crazy woman, huh?"

He started to say *stalker* was not right, but then he realized that in a way it *was* accurate, if not literally so. It *was* true that Sandra never gave him any peace. "Yes, that's it," he said. "She's kind of crazy. *Si!*" He wanted to give this man an illustration—the time Sandra had followed him around his apartment, trying to talk about a color scheme, something in mint green and cinnamon though he had tried to make it clear how desperately he needed to study his notes. She had disregarded his request for privacy the way a mother brushes aside a child's unreasonable demands. But he wasn't sure the man would understand all that, so he only said, "She won't leave me alone."

"A woman in love, eh?"

"No, I don't think so." This was an interesting idea. And foreign. He would have to think about whether or not Sandra loved him. She had never actually said so though sometimes she would affectionately rub the top of his head.

"Without a doubt a woman who follows you is in love, crazy or not." The waiter smiled, shrugged, and then left to take food to another table.

Stephen sipped his beer and turned his attention to the table with the pretty, talkative woman. He had always heard Hispanic women were submissive, but this woman was anything but. She interrupted the four men at the other table with loud protestations. "*No, no. No tienes razón,*" she said and went on to explain loudly something about a priest they seemed to be arguing about named *Alejandro*. "*Padre Alejandro,*" they kept saying. The talk seemed to be about whether or not he was a virgin. The men seemed to be saying most priests were *not* virgins and most were gay. As for Alejandro, the woman seemed to be insisting he had made a pass at her.

"*Increíble,*" the young man in the red shirt kept saying.

"*Sin sombre de duda. Muchas veces,*" she said.

"*Entonces no es homosexual,*" said a man with a paunch, who was wearing a gold cross. He seemed to be the ringleader. He had an elaborate beard, shaped like a *w* that was joined at the top, and he wore a gold earring. Stephen thought he looked piratical.

"*Es posible que es un bisexual,*" said the man in the red shirt. "*Pobre Alejandro. Marta . . .*" Stephen could understand nothing more, but the other men all laughed.

So the woman's name was Marta.

The man wearing the cross glanced Stephen's way and made some comment, obviously about him and the woman together, at which the other men laughed. Stephen fixed his gaze on the soccer game. He began to think about leaving, but he noticed the waiter was telling them something, and soon they began to give him pitying looks. Pretty soon the young, red-shirted man motioned for him to join them.

"Come on over," said the man with the cross. "We'll buy you a beer. Jaime, bring him another Corona."

Reluctantly, worrying that he could not return the favor, Stephen went to sit at their table while the waiter set down his third beer. This would be his last. Usually after three beers he began to feel less nervous around people, and now, with the beers and the fatigue from all the biking, he felt very relaxed, even though he sensed they were making fun of him. But he felt that wonderful physical tiredness deep in the muscle he had felt as a child right before sleep when he had played hard all day. He smiled at everyone in the bar, and everyone, including the three women, smiled back.

"How much you been riding your bike today, man?" one of the men asked.

Stephen did some calculations. "Oh, maybe fifteen or twenty miles altogether."

"Look at his thigh muscles in these shiny pants," Marta said. "Look at the arms on this guy." She got up and felt his right biceps, encircling his arm with her coral-nailed fingers. "Let me see those leg muscles up close. Stand up and turn around." One of the other women at the table, chunky with dark, curly hair, called out, "Put your hands on your waist and turn yourself. Like a model."

He hesitated but did as they said, grinning foolishly.

"Pay no attention to them," said the man with the cross. "They like to boss guys around. Especially Marta."

"Hey!" Marta leaned across the table and slapped the man hard on the shoulder. Her ponytail and earrings danced. "They like it too." She said something in Spanish.

"She's talking about your nice ass," said a small, quiet man, who was much older than everyone else—perhaps in his late sixties.

"I didn't say *nice*. I said *excelente*." Marta winked at Stephen.

The man with the cross was now looking at him sadly. A hand set another Corona down near the other, which, surprisingly, was over half gone. "How come a guy like you, a guy who is in marathons, lets a woman get to him. You tell her you don't want her following you."

"Hey!" shouted Marta. "What do you know? Maybe she has a right."

The two of them seemed to be having a feud.

"She's making him miserable," said the man with the cross. "Just look at him. You can see he's miserable. I once had a woman who kept calling me. Every day she called and said I didn't love her. She cried." The man rubbed his eyes and made loud weeping noises. " 'You don't love me anymore. You don't *make* love to me anymore.' "

"Yeah," said the man in the red shirt. "It was your wife." There was laughter throughout the bar. Stephen stared at the young guy's tattoo. Without his reading glasses on, he could not make out what was depicted—some kind of animal. It looked like a lizard or coiled rat.

"No, no man. It wasn't Paula. It was a crazy woman. You remember her, that red-haired one. She wasn't bad looking, but she was crazy. But you guys, you heard all this. She was stupid too. Listen, man." He turned to Stephen, grabbed his upper arm, and breathed into his face. "It was very fortunate she was so stupid. I told her I had a lawyer who was tapping the phone. I told her it was illegal in this country to call someone if they told you not to. She was new here, and she believed me, so she quit calling. But I had to stay away from church for a while."

Stephen stared at the man, trying to figure out if this could be true. Everyone else was laughing, so maybe it wasn't, but the man with the cross kept insisting it was. "Honest you guys. I wouldn't shit you."

"Yeah, yeah," said Marta. "Big guy." She turned to Stephen. "Hey, *culo excelente*, I know why your girlfriend is following you."

Stephen felt his face grow warm. "No, no," he said. "It's not that. She wants to control me." He added disparagingly, "She drives a Volkswagen."

"Trouble," said a late-fortyish man wearing a nicely-ironed denim shirt unbuttoned over a white T-shirt. He had a rather flat face and a beaky nose. He seemed to Stephen the most respectable of the four. "That is much, much trouble." He told a story almost entirely in Spanish, which he directed at Stephen, though Stephen caught practically nothing of it because the words were swimming past him. Something about *una mujer* and *una pistola*. The man made several cocked-finger hand gestures, pointing the *"pistola"* right, left, right, left, then knocked his "gun hand" with his other hand, and it seemed as if the woman might have taken several shots at him but missed because someone had deflected her aim. Stephen could not believe what he was hearing.

"*Es verdad?*" said the man in the red shirt, laughing.

"*No loco, no es verdad!*" said Marta. "He's full of shit." She rejoined her girlfriends.

"It's true," said the man who had told the story. "It was maybe ten years ago."

Marta pointed a coral-nailed finger at him. "Yeah, you were already old," she said. "I don't want to hear some story about some old guy."

"Forty-eight isn't old," said the man with the cross. "How old are you, kid?" Everyone stared at Stephen.

"Twenty-six."

"You look younger," said the older, quiet man. "I was also around twenty-six when something happened. I was married, but it didn't make no difference. This woman was crazier than that red-haired woman of his because she told my wife she loved me. She said they should share me."

"No way," said the man with the cross.

"You are all full of shit," said Marta.

The quiet man smiled at them. Instead of raising his voice, he lowered it as if he were ashamed. "My wife and I loved each other, so we talked about it. My wife said it was okay with her if it would stop that woman from following me around. She even followed me around the grocery store every Saturday."

"How come you were buying the groceries?" said the man with the cross. "You had a lazy wife?"

"No, no. We had little kids. My wife had to watch them, so I had to buy the groceries. No big deal."

"My wife takes the kids with her," said the young man in the red shirt.

"Your wife was the crazy one," Marta practically screamed at the man telling the story. "I wouldn't share no man. I would tell that woman a thing or two, and if she didn't listen, I would convince her." She shook a fist.

"I felt sorry for her, but I didn't want to do it with her. I tried to talk to her. I said I loved my wife, but she said she would wait because I would change my mind."

"Was she pretty?" asked the man with the cross.

"Not pretty, but okay."

"If she was okay, then you were the crazy one."

"*Dígame*," Stephen said eagerly. Everyone laughed, especially the man telling the story. He shook his head and his voice dropped even lower. "It has a sad ending. She died.

She died waiting. She didn't eat enough, and she got sick and died. My wife said I should have done it with her because she really was crazy, and I could have cured her."

"Yeah man, you should have cured her," said the man with the cross. "I would have cured her."

"I didn't want to."

"Then your wife was crazy too," Marta said. "You other guys talk about your crazy women, but this guy had two of them." She shook her head. The other women at her table laughed.

Stephen, a little drunk now, began to wonder if Sandra might not be some kind of crazy, but he could not imagine that she would ever get ill over it.

Marta said something in Spanish to her girlfriends, then turned back to the men. "You guys make it sound like following a man is the wrong thing. Sometimes it's necessary. But I tell you if I follow someone, I get him. He doesn't get away. And he likes it that way."

Stephen stared at her. He imagined her on a bicycle, pedaling faster and faster after him, and overtaking him. She would find him in the best hiding place. He imagined his leg muscles turning into concrete pillars. He would be astride his bike and part of him would want to flee from her, but he would be weighted and powerless, as incapable of movement as in a dream.

The waiter brought them all another round. As he placed the beer bottles on the table, he pointed the top of one at Marta and said, "If you stalk a guy, like this kid's girlfriend stalks him, you are crazy too."

"No, you're not!" She stood up and reached for her purse. Stephen didn't think he'd ever seen anyone prettier in his entire life. She had the most beautiful dark eyes and the most beautiful black hair. Her teeth were large and white, and he could not imagine that he would ever be able to escape her. But whatever would overtake him would be really something.

"There is nothing wrong with it. I'm here to tell you," she said loudly. "Sometime you got to watch a guy like a hawk!" Her two girlfriends were looking up at her. The chunky one said, "You tell them, Marta."

"Sting has a song about it," Marta said.

"Who is that?" asked the older, quiet man.

"You know. Sting. That old rock singer." She began to sing. " 'Every breath you take/ Every move you make/ Every bond you break. . .' " She wagged a finger at Stephen. " 'Every step you take/ I'll be watching you.' So you better watch it, big guy." She folded her arms and narrowed her eyes at him, while her girlfriends clapped and hooted.

"I got to go now. I got to go watch someone." She came closer to where Stephen was sitting and touched him on the shoulder. "But if I wasn't already watching a guy real close, I would be watching this guy with the good legs and the excellent ass." She leaned over and kissed him on the forehead.

"I'll walk out with you," said the man wearing the cross. "I'm going home."

"Yeah, you got to watch your wife," said the young guy in the red shirt.

"Funny guy."

Stephen stared after them as they paid. Through the window, he saw them get into separate cars and pull away.

"Don't look so sad," said the young man. "You don't want to mess with her. Take my word for it."

Eventually the other three men left, and Marta's friends as well. Stephen counted twenty-one empty beer bottles on the table. He had had five beers he thought, or maybe six.

He was so hungry he scraped leftover beans off a plate with his fingers.

When he was done eating their leftovers, he put his head down on the table and tried to imagine making love to the woman who had just kissed him. To imagine it he had to think of himself as a character in a movie where a man is swept away by a wild woman. They would make crazy, passionate love, and he would lose all timidity.

He had been living life all wrong. It was wrong to fret and stew about having to deal with someone like Sandra. He should be like the guys at the table—laugh it off or run (which he *had* done, come to think of it). Or maybe he would follow the example of the quiet man and simply explain that he just couldn't, even though bad things might result. He would tell Sandra he loved someone else, and really that was true— for the moment anyway.

"Be direct," he told himself. "*Directo.*" But he got up slowly, feeling an ache in his thigh muscles, those muscles the woman had just praised. He waved *goodbye* to the waiter and said *adios* in a voice that sounded so much louder than usual he startled himself. The waiter smiled and waved back. "*Adios amigo,*" he said.

He was tired, very tired. The night was closing in. He needed to think what to do, where to go. He could probably go stay at a motel somewhere and get his parents to let him use their credit card. There were several near the Plaza, or perhaps he could go back into the bar and ask the waiter. He was so distracted thinking where to go next, he nearly pulled out in front of a pickup truck, and he saw the young, dark-haired driver quickly remove his arm from his girlfriend's shoulder to toot his horn.

He might just stay a night or two. Meanwhile he would get his locks changed on the apartment. He would eventually need to explain, but he would do it quietly, dispassionately, like the quiet guy, and if that didn't work, he would laugh in Sandra's face. He had already run from her. That was something.

Yes, it was a scary thought, but he could do it. "I can do it," he said aloud but the sound of his voice was much quieter now. And when, a little later, he pedaled slowly back past the billboard advertising Volkswagens, he realized he was retracing the very same route, as if he were heading back to his little apartment.

He was so tired, and suddenly he felt he could no more prevail against Sandra if she was out to get him than he could against the woman in the restaurant, even though, in Sandra's case, it would be giving in to nothing. Pedaling back uphill, he felt as if his legs, his arms, his back, his whole body were turning to stone.

The Garrs

In the summer of 1976, just before my eighth-grade year, Carter-Mondale signs went up in our neighborhood. Our neighborhood, then, was full of Democrats, and for a little while it seemed we were all charmed by Jimmy's big grin and kind, worried eyes. It was a lower-middle-class/working-class area on Kansas City's east side. My parents' split level with its neatly clipped yew hedge and green lawn, which my father faithfully doped spring and fall with Scotts Weed & Feed, was one of the standouts.

Across the street and three houses down was a hunter-green house with a large oak shading most of the yard. The house had been losing its looks for several years now. A new family, named Garr, had just moved into the hunter-green house, and when I stepped out my front door to walk our fat, old terrier mix, all four members were outside putting up a Vote-for-Jimmy sign. My mother already had taken them her "famous meatloaf" though she'd left out the sausage. That was because the real-estate lady, a personal friend, had told her Mrs. Garr, and possibly the children, were Jewish. "Nice enough people though," said her friend.

My mother confirmed this assessment and said there was a girl my age and a boy a couple of years older.

That day Mrs. Garr held the sign while the son hammered it in. Mr. Garr stood beside them holding a level. They all had their backs to me except for the daughter, who sat on the front steps painting her fingernails. She gave a little wave when she saw me. Then the others came over to the curb to introduce themselves.

Mrs. Garr was a bit heavy in the middle, but the father and children had slight builds. The girl's name was Monica, and the boy's, Tim, after his father.

"What a nice old doggy," said Mrs. Garr. "What's his name? I see by his little schlong you have a boy there."

"Saggy." Embarrassed, I added, "Because of his fat pouches."

"God, Mother!" said Monica. Tim laughed and lit a cigarette. He was a dark-eyed, slouchy kid with a couple of overlapping teeth, maybe fourteen or fifteen.

"Spare me a cig, Son," said Mrs. Garr.

"Please tell us your name," said Mr. Garr, a pale little guy with light red hair and blue eyes. My mother's friend had said he was part Irish. He was comical looking with arms and legs that seemed overlong. His large head with its big nose reminded me of Mr. Potato Head, and his large mouth and wistful eyes, of Carter.

"Debby," I said. "My mother named me after Debbie Reynolds, but she spelled it with a *y* because it's not as cutesy."

"Fascinating," said Mr. Garr with a sweet smile.

"Do kids call you *Little Debbie*—like the pastries?" Tim asked.

"Don't pay any attention to my brother," said Monica. "And my mother is kinda blunt." She was extremely pretty, even with her chipped front tooth. She had dark, curly hair, deep-brown eyes, wide-spaced with thick lashes, and her father's fair skin. Where had she gotten her prettiness?

Perhaps from her mother, though it was hard to imagine. Mrs. Garr wore frumpy clothes and had frizzy, dyed-red hair, but, like Monica, she had nice dark eyes, only with dark circles beneath.

The family invited me in for a Coke, insisting I bring Saggy inside, where I saw many unpacked cardboard boxes in the living room and narrow hallway. Saggy sniffed around a bit and sprawled in a nest of crumpled newspapers under the coffee table.

"My parents are antiquers," Monica said. "Those boxes are full of junk for sale."

"Wheeler dealers," said Mr. Garr happily.

Mrs. Garr, a cigarette dangling from a corner of her mouth, poked around in a box, tossing out more newspaper. "We've peaked," she said morosely. "The antique market is on the wane, Debby. Too much goddamn competition."

Mrs. Garr looked older than her husband, and both looked older than my parents. Mrs. Garr might have been in her early fifties. The living and dining rooms were chock-full of old furniture. Pottery, glass, and metal toys cluttered the mantelpiece and two big bookcases. I stared at a what-not shelf holding small dishes that seemed to be tiny mosaics.

"Cloisonné," said Mrs. Garr. "We sell out of the house on occasion. I hope no one makes a stink."

I quickly made friends with Monica, and before long I was spending a lot of time with the Garrs, who seemed to me very unusual and interesting.

I came to see the Garrs as outsiders in our neighborhood. I mean by that that they were more serious, more aware. At least Mrs. Garr was. Because, as I learned from Monica, she had lived in New York once and had an accent and was Jewish, I thought of her especially as more perceptive.

And I thought of them as more apart. Behind their house was a woody area. In front was the big oak, and on the side large viburnums and forsythia run amok. It was as if they lived in a cottage in the woods. In front, junipers grew halfway up the walls. The inside had a musty smell that worsened in damp weather.

"It's because that creek to the east floods the basement when it rains. That's why they got it so cheap," my mother said.

I said her realtor friend had tricked them into the sale.

"No, Debby. It just means they don't pay attention when they should."

Mr. Garr was a now-and-then house painter, but since he avoided exteriors—he disliked heights—and fussed over the trim when he worked inside, he didn't make much.

They didn't spend much money on their house. Materials for redecorating projects came from bargains they picked up on their antiquing rounds. They'd found some wallpaper at twenty-five cents a roll and put it up in the pink, plastic-tiled bathroom—black-and-white cartoons of bosomy women dressed for a dance and men with swelled chests wearing top hats and tails. Our bathroom had beige ceramic tile with pale-blue flowers.

I loved their house. I loved all the "items," as Mrs. Garr called them. In the mint-green kitchen (not the avocado favored by my parents) were all sorts of oddities—old cookie and butter molds, heavy iron keys, a deer weathervane, candy scoops, a brass scale, an old bacon cooker, a stereoscope. Churns were now trash cans. There was a blue-and-white Dutch clock and a blue-and-white canister set with windmills and chunky Dutch children. The windowsill above the kitchen sink held small pieces of glassware in crimson, violet, orange, green, and various shades of blue. In the kitchen you could catch the light shining through all those colors.

More pedestrian things were piled into a dry sink, including a dented Drip-O-lator Mrs. Garr used to make her strong coffee. That smell, which I also loved, would usually cancel out the mold smell seeping up from the basement.

I heard the oddest words at the Garrs', words with an aura: *Hobnail, Heisey, Bohemian, Kewpie, Lalique, bisque, Baccarat, satin glass, majolica, delft.* They owned things I hadn't known existed: celery dishes, whale-oil lamps, goblets, cruets, moustache cups, fish knives, salt dishes, trivets, boot jacks, magic lanterns. Most of these things sat around with price stickers on their bottoms in case a customer might stop by, but few did.

"We're on the wane," Mrs. Garr would say. "Our heyday is past."

"Oh, we'll pick up," Mr. Garr would say.

"You're full of shit," she'd say. Mr. Garr hunched his shoulders when she answered him rudely.

Unlike me, neither Monica nor Tim took any interest in the items, but they had learned to tread carefully for fear of breakage. One day I bumped into an end table, causing a little Steuben glass bird to break a wing.

Mrs. Garr said in a cold voice, "You know I like you, Debby, but run on home and don't come back until you can be more goddamn careful." Tearful, I offered to pay her out of future allowances, but she rolled her eyes and waved a hand toward the door.

Hurt and miffed, I stayed away a week. It killed me that I had been exiled from the Garrs'.

My own parents used polite speech. They were fond of looking for the bright side and finding silver linings. I told

Monica and her mother I thought my parents had probably wanted someone exactly like Barbie. "Oh, Debby," Mrs. Garr said, "don't be so damn silly."

Her cursing kept me on alert, which, I thought, was not such a bad thing.

"Oh, Jimmy, you goddamn crazy nebbish, I'd like to slap you silly," she would say when she'd had enough of Carter's earnestness. But when Carter brought Sadat and Begin together at Camp David, she raved about "that beautiful man with so much soul in his eyes." After the accords, she hugged everyone. "There's hope in the world. There's hope!" she'd say.

She worried when Carter's popularity went into decline. "He's a nebbish, but at least he means well," she said. She made herself listen to his speeches whereas my parents turned off the television. "We need to hear this stuff," she said, "even though he makes me tired."

In the spring of '79 Tim was in his senior year. I heard from Monica he got teased a lot, probably because he dressed oddly and was skinny with bad teeth. One day it rained heavily, and Tim, wearing a black Prince T-shirt to school, happened to make a comment in the hall to a guy named Jason Lind, who was cussing Carter for his gas woes. "I can't get to my fucking job," Jason said.

"So get a fucking bike," Tim called out.

"It's raining, you fag jerk," Jason said.

Tim was with a guy named Ed Kleese, a nerdy kid with an adenoidal voice. Ed made the mistake of saying, "Who's a fag, you dumb asshole?" Jason sent his buddies to drag the two boys into the center of a circle where they were wrestled to the floor, de-pantsed, and left standing naked from the waist down except for their socks and tennis shoes. They retreated to an alcove where they removed their shirts to cover themselves. A couple of teachers rescued them but not before maybe forty or more kids caught a glimpse. Tim fought hard and came out with bruises on his arms and legs.

Unlike her brother, Monica was popular and had friends to console her. "Jason's a spaz," said Amy Lancaster. "Just let Tim talk about it," said Sarah Rooney. The school counselor called to apologize, but Mrs. Garr blew up. "What's wrong with you? You can't prevent kids from bullying other kids?" She talked of suing when she heard Jason only had to serve two weeks of in-school suspension. His cohorts got the same sentence, including a guy who lived six doors from me named Seth Johnson. Tim took to drawing revenge-fantasy cartoons. Jason and his buddies hung from a tree or had their heads severed by guillotines. Splashes of black blood flew in all directions.

"He hates the world," Mrs. Garr told me. "He won't walk down the street because he thinks it could happen again—with that awful Seth kid so close."

"I don't think he should be too afraid of Seth," I said. "It was Jason who got them going."

"But he went along with it, Debby. Don't be a dolt!"

"Those guys are just insecure," Monica said.

Seth's mother and my mother had done macramé together only last year, and for a while our house looked as if a huge spider had us in its web. After Monica moved in, we used to walk around the neighborhood, and sometimes we would come across the Johnson brothers. Seth would say things. "Hey, Little Debbie," he'd say. "I bet you taste good. Hey, Monica, you get your nose fixed?"

"It's *Debby* with a *y*," I'd yell back.

"Go fuck yourself," Monica would say.

"I'd rather do it with you, sugar lump. Right, Chris?" he'd ask his younger brother.

"For sure."

In the summer and fall of 1980, Reagan signs outnumbered the Carter signs. Our yard and the Garrs' had the only signs promoting Jimmy. Just after the election, Mrs. Garr came down with bronchitis, which she blamed on Reagan's victory. Every time she coughed, she cursed "that damn Hollywoodenhead." She wandered around the house drinking hot lemonade spiked with bourbon from a collectible Jim Beam bottle she was keeping until its resale value increased. Or she sat moodily at the Formica table in the kitchen drinking and smoking while she plugged away on an itemized list for an appraisal.

She did lots of appraisals now to help make ends meet. "I'm brilliant," she told me. "I'm quick, and I don't forget. I know the value of things."

In January Monica and I were listening to the inaugural address when Mrs. Garr stood up and yelled at the screen when Reagan said he wanted to get government off our backs.

"You want another Little Rock? You want *more* air pollution? Numbskull! You want babies that starve and old people to die without their medicine? You want big business to run without a leash?"

"Now, Hetta," said Mr. Garr. "He looks like a nice enough fellow."

Mrs. Garr grew red in the face. "Dolt! Nebbish!" she shouted. "He's going to undo everything FDR did. Kennedy! The War on Poverty!" She broke out coughing and left the room.

"She's crazy," said Monica. "She's driving me crazy. I can't wait to move out."

I stared at the fireplace mantel, noticing all the dust on the metal toys. I couldn't remember ever seeing Mrs. Garr clean house, though plenty of times I had seen Mr. Garr washing dishes with a tea towel tucked into his pants.

"Now, now," said Mr. Garr. Carefully he picked up the ashtray that Mrs. Garr and Tim, and sometimes I, used when smoking, dumped it into a churn/trash can, and wiped it out with a paper napkin. "She's overwrought because she's been working hard." Mr. Garr had the palest eyes and the bushiest eyebrows. In the light cast by the cheap pole lamp, his eyebrows looked nearly white.

"No," I said. "It's Reagan."

Tim stubbed out his cigarette and stared darkly at the TV set. "Mom's right," he said. "He looks like a dumb jock. Didn't he play one once?"

"He played Knute Rockne," Monica said.

"No, no!" I shouted. I always got loud when I knew I was right. "He played George Gipp. He's the one who died. Don't you remember?"

Tim sat up. "That's right. And he played that guy in *Kings Row* who lost his legs." He threw himself back on the couch and moaned, "Where's the rest of me? My legs! My legs! My dick! My whole fuckin' lower half is missing!"

I laughed. Monica said, "Tim, you're such a moron."

"He couldn't act for shit." Tim lit another cigarette. "My thesis is . . ."

"Who cares," Monica said.

"My thesis is a good actor might accidentally make a good president. But not a bad one."

"Go see about your mother," Mr. Garr told Monica.

"I'll go," I said.

Mrs. Garr was in the kitchen getting herself another hot lemonade with Jim Beam. "It soothes my throat," she said between coughs.

"I'll fix it. Sit down."

"You're a good girl, Debby. Your parents must be good parents."

"I guess. They're boring, though—not like you guys." I asked for a cigarette.

"There are worse things than boring. One is being a dolt. I won't name names, but I'm married to one. This country is full of dolts and schmucks, I'm sorry to say."

Gossiping with Monica later, I said I didn't think her mother had a good opinion of her father.

We were sitting on her front stoop, and the junipers had grown so big, we were almost entirely hidden from passersby.

"I'd trade you parents any day," Monica said. "I bet your parents would pay to get my tooth capped."

"Mine live in a dream world."

"But they're normal. I'll take normal any day."

When we were seniors, Monica started working part-time at Pizza Hut for pocket money. She and I were still friends, but since she had gotten in more and more with the popular kids, we weren't as close. We had once planned to go to KU and be roommates, but now she added, "If it works out."

I didn't see much of Tim either. He was going to Metropolitan Community College and delivering papers for the *Kansas City Star*. He shared an apartment with a guy who did cartoons for a little midtown newspaper.

For a while I went with a boy named Bill Chuff from my church youth group. When I told Mrs. Garr about him, she said, "I bet you're already saying, 'That's enough, Chuff.'"

We did it on the fifth date. I told a friend in the youth group, and the second person I told was Monica's mother, who said, "Two words, Debby: birth control."

Since her car had conked out, Mrs. Garr began paying me to drive her to appraisals in the used red-and-white Chevelle my parents had helped me make payments on. I would carry along a yellow legal pad. While she called out items and prices, I entered them in columns. If the print in a pricing book was too fine, I would look things up for her. One day we did an appraisal for a woman with a lot of Mary Gregory pieces. When the woman left the room, Mrs. Garr held up a vase and said, "I hate all this Mary Gregory dreck."

"It's kind of too pastel," I said. Actually, the vase was cranberry-colored, so I added, "I mean pastel in feeling."

"Victorian schmaltz."

I said I hated pastels. "I don't like the way Bill dresses," I said. "He wears his Levi's too high on the waist, and they always look so new."

"Is he Republican or Democrat?"

"He's a moderate Republican."

"There's no such thing. In this dopey country—which I love, don't get me wrong—the Democrats are the moderates. In my early days I was a socialist, sweetheart."

"Actually, he's undecided."

She gripped my arm. "Don't fall for a fence-sitter. Or make sure you can bully him. What would it be like to be married to some idiot who votes against the minimum wage? You'd go nuts." She sighed loudly and coughed a little cough that sounded like a gargle. "I hate to tell you, but I can see Monica turning out that way."

"Maybe she's going through a rebellious phase."

"Who needs it?" We returned to the Mary Gregory pieces. They showed an idyllic world where a girl or boy in a natural setting swung, fished, blew bubbles, or rolled a hoop.

"Pretty, pretty, pretty," she said.

I said I thought Monica and I had grown apart a little.

"She's pulling away from us too . . . She's not happy because we can't give her stuff."

"What kind of stuff?"

"Not-like-we-have-around-the-house stuff."

"She's a good kid," I said. "She'll come around."

After I graduated from community college, I commuted to KU thanks to a grant and loan package. On weekends, I still did appraisals with Mrs. Garr if Mr. Garr had a painting job. "You're better at it. He breaks more things than you ever thought about, Debby," she said, elbowing me in the ribs.

Monica decided to stay in town so she could work more hours. She'd impressed the faculty at a local Catholic university into giving her a scholarship. She confided she wanted to move out but couldn't afford to. Instead, she redecorated and painted her bedroom white. She'd picked up a Danish modern dresser at a garage sale and gotten rid of the old oak piece her parents had bought, taken up the worn-out oriental rugs, and replaced the curtains with white mini blinds, storing her old things in Tim's room since he had moved to New York.

Several months later, Mrs. Garr called to cancel out of an estate sale. She had come down with a terrible case of bronchitis and could barely talk. In a way I was glad not to have to listen to her hacking. On the other hand, I wanted to talk to her.

"It's a mold allergy," my mother said. "They should never have bought the house in the first place."

"It's not their fault!" I shouted. "It's a lack of government standards."

I wanted to talk to Mrs. Garr because my latest boyfriend had dumped me. I wanted to confide that the guy, Greg Burgess, was a minority person. His father was black and his mother, white, to be exact. I would have bragged to Monica, too, but she was away visiting Tim.

Greg was a couple of years younger, very smart, very good looking with light brown skin with a sort of golden tone to it. Unfortunately he had dropped me for a pretty black girl, who was several years younger than me. I wanted to tell Mrs. Garr I thought my animosity toward the girl showed I hadn't rid myself entirely of racism, though it was Greg who had dumped me for a pretty face.

The next weekend I went over to see her, taking her some flowers and a card I'd found with a bottle of Jim Beam on the front and the line, "Feeling run down? Don't neglect your medicine."

By late January she was up and running again, and we did several estate-sale appraisals that spring.

I floundered around in college trying this and that, dropping out to work, and eventually enrolling at KU Medical School to get a degree in nursing. Monica had graduated with a degree in marketing ("A BS," said Mrs. Garr. "Fitting.") and gotten a job as a manager of a Function Junction across town. She shared an apartment with a friend she'd met at college. My mother said she'd become "a real fashion plate." For a couple of years I saw little of her and less of Tim, though I still visited the Garrs, and Mrs. Garr kept calling me to help her with appraisals. Monica and I occasionally talked on the phone, always promising to get together when things got less hectic.

—◇—

The neighbors were complaining more and more about the Garrs' house. "I don't like to cast aspersions, but the house needs painting in the worst way," my mother said. "Also, they've got next to no grass in their yard because there's no sun, and have you seen how the vines are running over the gutters?"

I had noticed the interior was also pretty bad. Mr. Garr did keep the kitchen in fairly good shape, but if you looked into the corners in the living room, you'd find a bottle cap, maybe a scrap of newspaper, or old price stickers mingling with the dirt.

But in the spring of '88, I found Mr. Garr outside trimming bushes and tugging at the ivy and decided to help him a bit. Pulled back from the house, the ivy left little prints as if a small animal with claws had climbed all over the walls. Mrs. Garr stood in the doorway wearing an old pair of stretch pants and a flannel shirt and holding a cigarette. "Where are my rotten children when we need them?" she barked at me. "Come in and have a drink, Debby dear." It wasn't noon yet, but we had some Jim Beam and water and a smoke. I hadn't seen her in a while and thought she looked much older. The circles under her eyes had darkened. Outside in the daylight she'd looked pasty-faced; in the dark house, among her things, she looked better.

"You'll never guess what," she said. "Not in a million years."

"I know," I said. "Monica's engaged. She called me."

"Well, what's your opinion? Is he the cretin I think he is, or am I wrong?"

He was Chris Johnson, the younger brother of Seth, the one who had picked on Tim in high school.

I didn't know what to say. I'd always of thought of Chris as rather stupid, but he'd never been a bully. "I guess he's okay," I finally said. "I don't really know him that well."

Actually, a lot of people liked Chris. He was, I thought then, just an innocuous, sports-minded sort. From my mother I learned he had taught high school social studies a couple of years but hadn't liked teaching and was now working with a friend in construction. He and Monica had connected—or reconnected—through a mutual friend.

"That's the best you can do? Well, what do you think of this color?"

Mr. Garr had painted the kitchen baby blue.

"I coulda killed him, but he insisted. He had this paint left over from a job. He's on a tear now because that woman down the street said we needed to . . ." She tried to stifle a cough and was unable to finish her sentence.

"Mrs. Lyle? She's a bitch. You ought to see a doctor," I said.

"I will, I will. I've got an appraisal for us next weekend, Debby sweetheart. I'll be better by then. My husband"—she rolled her eyes—"has been helping me out, but you're so much better. He's so slow. He drifts along, talking about nothing to the customer." She imitated her husband's soft voice. "Nice figurines you got there, ma'am." She took another sip of bourbon.

That summer I moved in with a guy I met at KU, who was planning to be a pediatrician. I liked him because he seemed to want to be a good doctor. He was neither into the greed thing, nor was he like the phony liberals who said they wanted to help the poor, but you knew that feeling would last a year, if that. My boyfriend was into curing illness. Also, he was kind. So I was proud of him. Mrs. Garr was so happy when I told her that he came from a family of Democrats, who all expected Dukakis to win. I wasn't so sure. Dukakis seemed too nice—like Carter.

"Don't worry," Mrs. Garr said. "Dukakis is going to kick Bush's tush, but if he doesn't, it's not such a big deal. Bush's got *one-term* written on that solid-gold forehead."

Chris and Monica had a Vegas wedding and moved to Springfield, Missouri, so Chris could start a construction company with a buddy. Around the first of October there was a pitiful little reception at the Garrs', in spite of Monica's having talked them into buying a magnificent cake with three layers and supporting pillars. Mrs. Garr had just been diagnosed with lung cancer, so everyone was in a somber mood. She had decided to postpone treatment until after the reception.

My parents attended, along with a few other neighbors, some of the Garrs' antique-dealer friends, a couple of Monica's and Chris's friends, and of course the bride and groom. My new boyfriend was too exhausted from working around the clock in emergency to come. Chris's parents were not in attendance since they had flown to Houston to visit Seth, who had married the weather girl on a local station. They were expecting their first child. Tim flew in for the weekend.

"I never thought the Johnsons were unkind," my mother said, "but this seems uncalled for. Is it because Monica has Jewish blood, I wonder?"

"Blood is blood," I said, speaking with authority because of my doctor boyfriend.

At the reception, after Monica relayed the details of her Vegas wedding, no one had much to say. Chris stared longingly at the quiet TV set. The Garrs had made the mistake of having the reception on Sunday afternoon when the Chiefs were playing.

Eventually Monica took her mother into the kitchen where Mr. Garr and I were fixing plates of cake and ice cream. "Would you mind if Chris watches TV in the back room?"

Mrs. Garr shrugged.

Shortly after Mrs. Garr began her chemo, Tim flew back again. He now had braces, but they made his sneer more pronounced. He told me he had decided to move back home "until Mom bites the dust." "It's going to happen, Debby darlin'. Death is going to pay a call. It's in her brain too, y'know."

"My mother told me. How's she holding up? How are you doing?"

"Me? Not so good. It's goddamn gruesome." He told me in New York he had worked at odd jobs while trying to write plays. He had made friends with people in off-off-off Broadway and had a script accepted, but the only thing to materialize was that his play would be performed in some rich person's loft.

He was also contributing pieces to a "satiric little rag." I didn't find the columns he showed me all that funny. Most of his topics had to do with everyday life, maybe something about dog turds or trick-or-treaters or trash collectors, but his writing made you think that dogs, trick-or-treaters, and trash men were all urban agents of the devil, existing only to make our lives unremittingly miserable.

I visited Mrs. Garr several times, dreading the visits because she was going downhill. Her skin looked ashy; her sunken eyes seemed to shine out of twin wells. Once or twice when Mr. Garr went to tackle an estate sale on his own, I drove her to the hospital for her chemo. She was pretty chipper through it all. Once she told me excitedly, "I met an old lady in there who used to correspond with Eleanor."

"Eleanor?"

"Rigby," she said with a guttural laugh. "Roosevelt. God, Debby, what other Eleanor?"

Monica called me to say she was coming home, but then she backed out. Her car was in the shop. Later, she said she couldn't deal with it and not to hate her. She would explain later. "Anyway, Dad says he and the hospice lady are holding down the fort."

Tim was furious at her. "She needs to get her ass up here."

I thought it was pretty bad that she wasn't there. "I hope she gets here soon," I said to Mr. Garr. "I'd like to see her."

"So would I," he said wistfully. "She says she has a surprise for us."

I began to agree with Mrs. Garr that her husband was sort of a dolt.

Eventually we heard she was finally coming, and I found myself at the Garrs' house again, filled with dread, awaiting Monica's arrival. Tim had called earlier to say, "Come on over, Debby. The Wasp is about to buzz in."

Mrs. Garr was sitting in an easy chair with a little Jim Beam and water in a glass nearby. The doctor had okayed it, saying it would relax her.

As soon as Monica was out of her Chevy Suburban, we saw she was pregnant—maybe five months along. I hadn't picked up on it at the reception, but it was obvious now with her big over-blouse and the pants with a stretchy panel.

"Holy shit! What sex is it, the little chip off the old block in there? Or do you know?" Tim patted her stomach.

"A boy. I just had a sonogram," she said proudly. She smiled at all of us. Her face had gotten fleshier and was not so pretty as before. But her hair, in a sleek, short bob, looked very nice.

"You look like Betty Crocker with a bump," Tim said.

She was not amused, especially when Tim started referring to the baby as John Wesley. It seemed that Monica, like her husband, was now a Methodist.

"Monica, you're blooming," said Mr. Garr. "You're more radiant than ever."

"Thanks, Daddy. I had lots of nausea for a while. That's why I couldn't come up for so long. Mom and I wouldn't have been any help to each other." She kissed him on the cheek.

Mrs. Garr frowned at her daughter and was silent.

"How are you feeling, Mom? I brought you a macrobiotic diet book."

"All right." Mrs. Garr was wearing a blond wig, which she had bought as a lark—or maybe to get a rise out of Monica—but Monica didn't mention it.

Monica had stopped off at several stores and bought a wild assortment of food. Tim, Mr. Garr, and I stood around in the kitchen as she hauled out a package of brown rice, Kudos granola bars, Eggo whole-wheat waffles, canned carrot and apple juices, whole-wheat bread, Beanee Weenees, and a package of health cookies called C-biscuits.

Mrs. Garr tasted one and made a face. "Grainy," she said.

Mr. Garr had taken over as chief conversationalist, but he was awkward in the presence of his wife, and so turned to his daughter with question after question about the baby as Mrs. Garr watched from the recliner, tucked in a quilt, her feet in slipper socks sticking out awkwardly. When I patted a foot, she rolled her eyes.

"And you say you're feeling better these days, Monica?" her father asked. For the first time I noticed a lilt in his voice.

"Yes, much."

"Isn't she just beautiful?" he said. "You're the picture of health. When you had your sonogram, did you see the heart beating?" He turned to his wife. "Wouldn't that be exciting?"

"Yes," she said quietly. She seemed stymied by her daughter's condition. She looked down at a small plate of food I had made her and pushed the plastic fork around a little.

"Could they tell if he's grown a Chiefs' uniform yet?" Tim said.

"Funny," said Monica.

In response to her father's questioning, she told us she'd joined the Springfield Junior League and volunteered at the library as a literacy mentor. She was helping put on a charity benefit dance. Chris was thinking about running for city council, and if that worked out, maybe running for state representative.

"That's wonderful," said Mr. Garr.

"Running as what?" said Mrs. Garr.

"The city council's a nonpartisan election," said Monica with a little note of satisfaction.

"Okay, but what is he?"

"An independent."

"Why can't he be a Democrat? His parents are Democrats even if they forgot it when they voted for old lame brain. By the way, there's talk he can't . . ." Mrs. Garr made a little huffing sound and covered her face.

Tim picked up the thread. "They say he's had little strokes."

"Take it easy, Mom. I'm just saying . . . what I'm saying is . . ."

"What *are* you saying?" Eyes watering, Mrs. Garr stared hard at her daughter.

"You can't get anywhere in southern Missouri today if you're a Democrat."

"I don't believe that!" Mrs. Garr punched her plate with the plastic fork.

"Now, now. Don't upset yourself, Hetta," said Mr. Garr. "We shouldn't fuss at one another. Your daughter's having a baby. We should be happy."

She waved her hand to brush his voice aside, but the gesture was feeble. "At least I hope to God you won't support that fool Ashcroft."

"Can't we talk about something besides politics?" Monica said. "I came all this way."

"Call her Daniel Boone," said Tim.

"Oh, for God's sake." Monica got up from the table. "Let's go for a walk, Debby," she said.

We made our old loop through the neighborhood, passing the Johnson house. "I should have stayed with my in-laws," Monica said, "but she's never liked me much. *He* likes me all right. So does Seth."

"How do Tim and Seth get along these days, considering what happened in high school?"

"Seth apologized. He was just being juvenile, but Tim can't let it go."

Not *cruel*, I noticed. Not even *clueless*. *Juvenile*. I didn't know what to say.

She asked me what kind of nursing I was going into.

"I'm not sure. Maybe critical care—if I can take it."

"Is that why you don't mind being around my mother? She looks terrible. I can hardly stand to look at her. She's so thin. And the house . . . it's gone more downhill." She squared her shoulders. "Getting away . . . it's been good for me. I never knew how negative my mother was until I left."

We fell silent. I said, "It's hard. I see your mom on weekends sometimes."

"You should have been her daughter. You even have a Jewish name. *Deborah* means *bee*, or did you already know that? My name isn't really Hebrew. It's like Mom thought Tim and I would be lightweights. Sometimes I can't stand my brother."

"I was named for Debbie Reynolds," I said. "You know."

"Why won't Dad get his teeth fixed?"

"Money," I said. Monica didn't seem to have the simplest understanding of the simplest things.

"What a sweetheart. If it weren't for him, I probably wouldn't come home." We were now about two-thirds of the way through our walk and headed up a steep hill.

"I need more aerobic exercise," I said to break the silence. "And I'm going to quit smoking."

"Yes," she said. "Don't end up like Mom."

I thought she meant the cancer, but she said again, "She was always so negative about life."

"Well, maybe, but she cares about things." My voice sounded stern. Her remark made me angry, but I didn't want to start a fuss, so I was quiet. I was glad to get back to the house. I hugged them all goodbye and went across the street to my parents'.

"Well," said my mother. "How are they over there?"

"Not great."

Mrs. Garr died in early February of '89. Her last weeks were peaceful overall. I thought the election would make her feel down because Bush had badly defeated Dukakis, but she said, "It's better than having Reagan. Mr. Fat Cat Bush won't capture all those foolish hearts."

Until her death, Tim stayed home with her, and Monica returned a time or two. By then Mrs. Garr had quit trying to argue politics with her daughter and turned her attention to me.

"Don't give up on her, Debby. Maybe she'll get some sense. I'm asking God for it. Maybe she'll get tired of "—she said with a sneer in her voice—"Springfield."

Mrs. Garr had told her husband, "Forget the funeral, but a little memorial service would be okay." It took place a couple of weeks after her cremation. I brought my boyfriend, "Dr. Ted," and took Mr. Garr a bouquet of flowers and a sack of beautiful old marbles I'd found at a huge estate sale. Some of the marbles were quite old: some were agate, some handmade. They were all colors—beautiful greens and blues, some crimson and orange.

I had expected the occasion to be somber, but when I arrived, the place had been cleaned up by a housekeeping service hired by Monica. She had gotten her brother to box up a lot of the old items for sale. There was a brand-new matching sofa and set of chairs in a floral pattern, purple irises against a cream background, painfully new and bright against the worn wood floors.

Many of Mrs. Garr's antiquing cronies showed up. Chris's parents were there and my own parents and several other neighbors. There were big platters of ham and roast beef, and lots of snacks from a wholesale club, and in the kitchen, a big open bottle of Jim Beam, a bottle of Scotch, and one of vodka. Mr. Garr was in the kitchen fixing drinks for everyone.

Monica abstained, but Tim was wasted. He told me he had been there when "just like Blanche DuBois, she had a gentleman caller. With a fuckin' scythe," he added, staring down at his drink.

He had won a playwriting contest, and his play might, if the financing went okay, be performed off-off Broadway. He called it an "anthropomorphic comedy." The characters were trees with personalities—a macho, straightforward oak; a sentimental, intuitive willow; a neurotic aspen, and so on.

"What happens is the trees comment on different subjects," he said, "like the environment, politics, more personal stuff. A lot of it's parody. The oak and willow have lines that are supposed to suggest *My Dinner with Andre*." He sighed. "I wish Mom could've seen it."

"That's great, Tim."

"But Debby, I'm worrying about the critics saying stuff like *roots don't go deep* and shit like that."

"Even if they do."

"Yeah."

We watched Monica move around slowly, mingling with the guests. She chatted with her mother's antiquing cohorts, women with shrewd eyes and lots of jewelry; probably they were discussing the estate sale. She bragged about her brother's success in an "off-Broadway" production, pushing him a step closer to fame. Chris seemed in awe of her, even of Tim.

Mr. Garr also had a lot to drink. Even though I had given him the marbles half an hour ago, he was still showing them off to people and was chattering away. "Would you just look at these wonderful agates," he said to a very old lady standing next to me. "Some of them are handmade. Have you ever seen a more beautiful blue-green? Hetta would have loved them. She was crazy about beautiful things." Tears came to his eyes. He gave me a sloppy kiss on the cheek and then showed them for the second time to a severe-looking old woman in black.

The old lady, a Mrs. Lawrence, later whispered to me, "Hetta would have sold them in nothing flat if she could have."

"Oh, I don't know," I said. "She loved her 'items.' "

"Certainly, dear, but she never forgot for a minute what they'd bring."

Monica went into the kitchen and brought back a plate of chocolates to pass to the mourners.

Tim watched his sister, then, following Monica's new rules, went outside to smoke.

Mr. Garr drew near again to say he had a box of glassware he wanted to give me in the kitchen. "There's some green glass, Debby, maybe Honesdale or crackle glass. I can't remember." I tried to recall the Garr kitchen as it had been when I first met them and seen all that bright glass in the windowsill above the sink.

He took a long sip of his drink. "We were always so fortunate to have such wonderful things. Didn't we have beautiful things?"

"Yes," I said. "You did. You did." But I thought that Mrs. Garr might have said, "We're on the wane" or "look at what we've come to."

He gave me a big, sad-eyed smile, which reminded me again of Jimmy Carter, whose brother, Billy, had also died not long ago of cancer.

"Beautiful, beautiful things," he said. "Such riches!"

Brighton Green

Ricky Solis was weeding his small vegetable garden, stopping now and then to stare through his strange neighbor's rusty chain-link fence at five dogs lazing beneath a pin oak in her backyard. On his side, bees buzzed a large rose of Sharon near the fence. He couldn't decide if he liked the shrub. He had always thought it a showy, blowsy plant, but he'd decided to keep it since it mostly hid a section of her awful fence where a gate had been replaced with a piece of scrap sheet metal clumsily wired in place. At one time there must have been a passage into his yard, but now it was blocked.

Because the neighbor failed to keep up with all those dogs, the backyard was nearly grassless, a mucky, smelly mess. Depending on the wind direction, the dog-poop smell was a major or minor annoyance. He'd described the permeating odor of dog to his friends: "It's like something foul burning. Like sitting in a hot closet full of dirty socks."

The back door opened, and the woman, wearing old denim trousers and a gray sweatshirt, appeared on the wood staircase carrying a sack of dog food and assorted plastic bowls. A furious woofing and yipping began as the dogs rushed toward her: a big black Lab mix, a medium-sized, reddish-blond dog with pale eyes, a white-and-rust-colored dog that seemed a good part Brittany, and two little ones: a fuzzy-haired gray thing and a fat, dark-brown terrier mix. He shouted, "How's it going?" but his neighbor either didn't hear or chose to ignore him.

He had moved into this two-block development with its Britishy name, *Brighton Green*, about a year ago. It was located in an old inner-ring suburb with generally quite nice houses, mainly three bedrooms but a few larger, all the lots well kept, except for his neighbor's. Her house was to his south. North of Ricky was a vacant lot, where, he'd learned, a house had burned down ten years ago and not been replaced. Because of the empty space, it felt as if he and his neighbor were geographically separated from the other houses.

Her house was in terrible repair. Someone had started to repaint and stopped: the back was rust-red while the front was a faded medium brown. The neighbor herself was a dismal-looking person who kept to herself and only spoke to her dogs. He had heard various stories: that she was depressive, paranoid, that she had once killed a raccoon about to attack one of her dogs, that she likely sold the strays to a research lab to supplement her income.

"She's got a nephew that comes over," said the mean-spirited little gray-haired widow, who lived across the street. "If you ask me, he needs to get her into a *home*."

This conversation had taken place after the little widow, Cecilia Ostergren, summoned Ricky when one of the woman's dogs got loose, the fuzzy, gray one.

At Cecilia's bidding, Ricky carried the squirming dog across the street to the woman's front porch and knocked on the door. The porch was utterly devoid of amenities: no plants, not even artificial; no porch swing or chairs; no welcome mat. To his left some ancient, gangly, unpruned shrubbery with thin, desiccated leaves grew halfway up the window. Behind it dingy mini blinds with missing slats blocked the dirty picture window. A section of guttering hung below the porch ceiling to his right.

She opened the door and stared at him from heavy-lidded eyes. Her dark clothing was covered in dog hair. He nattered on, saying he had planned to introduce himself before. His name was Ricky Solis and what was hers?

"Gail Hoag," she muttered. She took the dog from him and did not say thanks. The other neighbors, excepting Cecilia, were a glad-handing, good-natured sort with yards of plentiful oaks and maples, yews and forsythia, and flower beds and fescue. Despite or because of his own house's isolation, he had taken it upon himself to frame his entryway with two Alberta spruce in tall blue glazed pots. But it seemed overreach to do more, considering Gail Hoag's house.

When he first moved into the neighborhood, he had just got through some unhappy times due to certain changes in his life and had been hit harder than expected. He was fifty-eight, so he could no longer think of himself as young by any stretch. For one thing, he had discovered, by comparing himself with more successful younger artists, that he was definitely not a natural. He should have known taking a plunge—from a very good job as a commercial artist into the real arts, in his case, sculpture—was ill-advised. A couple of terrible reviews had settled that.

Secondly, he had come out. He and his wife had divorced, and then his lover had left him. So he had retreated a little, from his city loft, to this suburb and to a full-time job managing a company that sold wedding supplies. If he could not be an artist, at least he could be artful.

Actually, he had already learned Ms. Hoag's name from a woman named Betty Wilson, another widow, the opposite of Cecilia, plump and bright-eyed. The deep green loveliness of early May had given him new heart, and he'd started walking in the evenings, trying to make a few friends. But most of his new neighbors seemed preoccupied. They had already formed their friendships, and he was late to the party.

Then he hit it off with Betty, who had glommed onto him right away. Later she would say they were kindred souls. The first evening she'd met him, she'd led him into her backyard to show off her two dogs, a heavyset yellow Lab named Silkie, who lounged beneath a crepe myrtle, and a good-sized, part-German shepherd, Heidi. Betty also had three cats, all named for her favorite minor character in Jane Austen—Lady, Catherine, and a male, de Bourgh. De Bourgh was "off on his evening odyssey."

She showed him her backyard cottage garden, and Ricky easily won her over by admiring her daylilies, clematis, hollyhocks, mallow, and foxgloves, even the garden art, "a hell of a lot of kitsch," she said. She was, so far anyway, the most likeable Brighton Greener he had met.

"I love kitsch," he said. She smiled and gave him a knowing look, as if she guessed his secrets. She brought out iced tea, and they sat chatting in old Adirondack chairs, Betty in loose Capri pants and a blue cotton shirt and Ricky in Bermuda shorts and sandals, like two Florida retirees.

"What do you know about the woman to the south of me? She's very strange."

"Gail Hoag? Not a lot. No one knows much. She used to drive, but I think now everything is brought to her by a man in an SUV—maybe a nephew. I doubt if she has kids."

Betty's chin stood out against her plump face and neck like a knob and went in and out as she talked. "That house drives the neat freaks crazy. She takes in stray dogs. She's got way over the limit, doesn't she?"

"I saw five."

"Maybe some died, and she buried them in that woody area behind her house," Betty said.

"Interesting," Ricky said absently. "I can picture her hauling a dog carcass back there. She's kind of ghoulish actually." Somehow, he felt vaguely disloyal saying this, though he did not know the woman at all.

Betty remained his favorite, though he had once said he would never make friends with anyone who owned unicorns in any form, and Betty had a sizeable collection in a bookcase. Usually they indicated a new-ager, yet Betty didn't seem that sort. One night, after two glasses of sherry, she told him she thought she kept the unicorns because they were phallic. Well, not the crystal one standing beneath a horrible rainbow canopy. It was a present from her granddaughter, so she had to display that one.

She had taught high school English. She was well read and prided herself, he could tell, on being well versed in politically- and geographically-correct terminology. Her son, she said, was married to a Latina. A neighborhood couple had recently returned from the Czech Republic. But she also liked a dirty joke and told one he'd already heard about a bulimic hooker. Her word for herself was *earthy*, which seemed a stretch, but if she wanted to think of herself that way, why not? He liked her. He was comfortable with her.

One night in late June she had him over for a supper of beef Stroganoff and salad. When he entered her house, the aroma made his stomach growl. Silkie and Heidi were hanging out in the kitchen. Betty poured glasses of Shiraz. She had swept back her white hair on one side. Ricky told her she looked fetching, and she blushed pink. She proposed a toast to themselves as "two eccentrics, two people on the fringe."

"Maybe," Ricky said, smiling.

She obviously liked him, and there was not such a huge difference in their age—maybe she was older by eight or ten years. He supposed he could give her a roll in the hay, but it would not be wise, nor did he want to. He soon knew her well enough that he should be able to tell her about coming out, but he sensed it might spoil things. No, the best thing to do was to be outrageous. He affected a German accent and said, "You're divine, Schatzi," and, leaning over, gave her a kiss on the cheek. Though she must know about him, she blushed with pleasure.

She suggested they take their coffee outside. When Betty hailed several neighbors, Ricky felt she was showing him off. Here in her backyard was a younger man with a small moustache wearing a Hawaiian shirt.

She phoned the forty-something couple next door, the people with Brighton Green's showiest house, best-kept yard, most trees circled with mulch, the only house with a bubbler in the birdbath.

"Lance is the president of the neighborhood association, but Michelle calls the shots. I know they absolutely hate my yard. Too formless, too . . ." Betty gestured toward clumps of zebra grass bent to the ground. "I should tie all that up."

Lance was replacing a dimmer switch, but Michelle said she would be right over. She gave a little wave before she came through the gate, wearing a bright purple shirt and crimson belt. She grasped Ricky's hand and squeezed it firmly. Ricky had guessed both Griffins to be in business; Michelle looked like she sold real estate. But she handed him a card with a cross below her name and below that *Certified Christian Counselor*.

"Actually I'll counsel anyone," she said, "even atheists, though I doubt an atheist would come to me since I apply Christian principles." She ruffled her hair, which was streaked different shades of blonde. The purple blouse had a little open circle between the top and second buttons and showed about an inch of cleavage.

He stared at her tanned forearm. Her purple-enameled nails tapped against the arm of her chair. He tried to think what to say. He might bring up recent Supreme Court decisions, but he guessed she might be pretty conservative, and he liked to avoid creating ill will if at all possible.

With his big toe, Ricky absently scratched the ribs of the big yellow lab, Silkie. He listened to the intermittent *ch,ch,ch* as the Griffins' sprinkler shot water through the barberry hedge into Betty's lawn.

"We missed you at Brightonfest last year, Ricky," Michelle said.

"I was probably out of town."

"Well, you just *have* to come this year. Betty and the committee go all out. Wonderful, wonderful food. Super, super decorations. Last year Betty made the cutest papier-mâché Christmas ornaments for everyone."

"You're working on my self-esteem," Betty said.

"Maybe I'll fix my mother's streusel," he said.

"Oh, is she German?" Michelle asked.

"Was. She passed away three years ago."

"The name *Solis* is Hispanic, isn't it?"

"My grandfather was Mexican."

Both women sighed. Fireflies blinked nearby. The three chatted on in a soft, halting way and somehow found themselves talking about the neighbor. "She obviously has clinical depression," Michelle said. "It's sad."

"Can the Bible actually help people with serious mental illness?" Ricky asked Michelle.

"Of course. The New Testament tells us we have a reason to live. And that, Ricky, is what all depressed people want to hear."

After another twenty minutes, Michelle got up. "I better get back to Lance. Don't laugh, but we have our couple time together."

"Oh, she's so full of it," Betty said when Michelle was out of hearing. "She turned in your neighbor to the city a couple of years ago."

A mosquito whined somewhere to Ricky's right.

Betty leaned closer. "I love it when it stays light so late. It's paradise to me. Can you smell the Asian lilies?"

From time to time he had noticed a sweet smell, and now that Betty brought the lilies to his attention, he noticed how powerful the smell was, almost cloying. He couldn't say he preferred it much to the ripe, tarry smell that drifted in from his neighbor's yard. Both caught at the throat.

Throughout August, spiders hung their webs throughout his garden. A thin filament stretched from a tree to a fence post at least fifty feet away. Monarchs made their way south, dropping down onto his Autumn Joy sedum before resuming flight. One morning he watched the little, fuzzy, gray dog snap at one, and Ricky saw orange wings fluttering in a circle on the ground.

"Damn dogs!"

But not long after, at Betty's prompting, Ricky acquired a dog of his own from the Humane Society, a strange, disproportionately shaped dog. Its thick red fur, mottled purple tongue, and small mane might come from chow genes, its stumpy legs and longish tail, from basset. He named it *Elmer*. Elmer gave him a reason to call his children, whom he had not spoken to in a while. His son had little to say, but his daughter, a sweet, liberal-minded girl, said, "I love the name."

"What else is going on in your life?" Suzi asked him. "Anyone new besides Elmer?"

"No one—of any persuasion." Then, for some reason, instead of mentioning Betty, he began to talk about the strange woman next door. "She's pretty much a persona non grata."

"I can see why."

"Yes, of course. But you can't help feeling sorry for her."

"Maybe you should contact social services."

"I don't like to report people."

"You don't have a thing for her, do you? Is she attractive?"

"Good grief, no."

That evening he lay on his leather sofa, watching Dr. Oz and drinking wine. He wished Betty would call and invite him for coffee. Last time she had served a lemon tart with a generous spiral of whipped cream. Again he considered bedding her. "She's too old," he said to Elmer. "Anyway, I'm not interested. And those unicorns."

Yet his own house was so austere. He had wanted it to look undecorated, natural. But he saw there was no life, especially in the living room with its old braided rug, brown leather sofa and chairs, bookcases, books, a television. So much brown. He felt dull. "Brown study," he said aloud. The television show did not interest him in the least. He really should call Betty and force an invitation. She must be lonely too.

He rolled onto the edge of the couch, and, tugging Elmer by the collar, dragged him up onto the couch beside him in order to lie with his arms around the dog. Elmer struggled, but Ricky grasped him tightly and spoke soothingly, stroking his back: "Quiet, Elmer, quiet." Elmer gave him a wary look, lifting an eyebrow, and lay still a moment before squirming free.

"Lonely," he said, "I'm terribly lonely." Tears came to his eyes. He saw that people like Michelle and Lance Griffin and Cecilia made life difficult for people like himself and his neighbor. You had to always be on the straight and narrow around them. Life was hard enough without having to live among the disapproving.

"I'll talk to her. I will. We'll be friends, allies."

Besides, he had a practical reason to seek her out. The big black dog had started growling and rushing the fence whenever Elmer came outside. If Elmer saw him, he would turn tail and run back in. Twice Ricky caught him pissing on the braided rug, so now he tied Elmer up several times a day in front. Unfortunately, one day Cecilia was outside pruning her lone forsythia within an inch of its life, and Elmer chose that time to walk as far as chain would allow, curbside, and hunker down.

Cecilia pointed the pruners at Elmer as if she would like to run him through and said, "Who wants to see *that*! *That* belongs in the back."

But before he took up the problem with his neighbor, it might do to court her a bit. He had always been good at courtship.

The next Saturday he picked five nice green peppers and a couple of tomatoes, Celebrities, a bit spotty but tasty nonetheless. It took him nearly an hour to work up his nerve and become the Ricky Solis he became at work, a jolly, chatty man capable of ignoring all sorts of irritations, setbacks, and hostilities.

Her doorbell didn't work, so he knocked. Immediately a din arose inside, a deep, steady, *woof woof* punctuated by *yips* and *arfs*. He heard her command the dogs to hush, then the unlocking of the chain. The door opened partway, and she stared out at him. He smiled back then looked away.

She wore her hair pulled back into a low ponytail. Her face looked sallow, wider at the bottom and jowly. Her nose was large, her mouth, pinched. Her only halfway good feature was her eyes—large and wide-set, a sorrowful brown.

"Yes?" she said in her low, sullen voice.

"I'm your next-door neighbor, Ricky Solis," he said quickly.

"We've already met."

"Anyway, I wanted to bring you these." He held out a white sack. "The peppers turned out pretty well. The tomatoes have a few spots, but if you just cut them off . . ."

A minor skirmish was going on at her feet. He looked down at her denimed legs, which blocked several small dogs: he saw brown and gray fur, wet black noses, little clacking paws, scratching at the doorsill. He heard another *woof* from behind the soiled blinds, saw them separated by the nose of the big black dog, whose large black head appeared. He and the dog frowned at each other, and the dog tossed its head and narrowed an eye.

His neighbor shoved the little dogs back with a foot. "Back! Get back!"

The scrabbling, yipping little dogs, the whole situation suddenly seemed comic to Ricky. "I see I got them going."

Not a smile. Not a nod. "I need to shut the door," she said. "Thank you." She held the sack before her a moment as if she wanted to hand it back. After the door shut, he realized he hadn't brought up the problem with Elmer.

After several more days of watching out for Cecilia and having to tether Elmer in front and stay with him so he didn't yip, he grew irritated. One cool morning when he saw his neighbor come outside to feed the dogs, he went up to a part of the fence where she could see him and called, "Ms. Hoag. Could I have a word with you?"

She stopped, put a hand to her forehead and turned, and slowly came his way.

This time, he was the polite-but-firm Ricky, who had recently told his young secretary, "If you keep making all these personal calls, I'll have to let you go."

"There's a small problem," he said. She frowned and blinked. The lower part of her face, beneath an old cloth hat, was in full sun. Her pale lips opened to say something, and he saw her teeth were very yellow.

"What is it?"

He explained the problem with the big black dog as cordially as possible.

"Henry?" she asked wearily.

"I guess. I was just wondering if maybe somehow you could get Henry to accept my dog." He heard a certain winsomeness enter his voice. "Would you mind helping me out?"

"All right," she said. "Wait here." She went inside and brought out a big choke chain attached to a leash, and, commanding the black dog (*Sit, Henry!*) slipped the leash over the big glossy black head. "Go get your dog," she said.

He brought Elmer out on a leash, but as soon as his dog understood he was being led to the fence, he tucked his tail beneath his legs and braced himself, so Ricky picked him up and held the struggling dog in his arms. "It's all right, right, Elmer," he said. "It's all right."

The reddish-gold dog with yellow eyes paced the fence, barking excitedly. "Hush, Sally! Hush, I said," his neighbor said. When the black dog snarled, causing Elmer to rake Ricky's neck with his claws, she tightened the dog's chain until he coughed.

"Oh, don't choke him!"

"Set your dog down," she commanded. He set Elmer down on the ground, but immediately Elmer tried to trot away. She knelt and loosened the big dog's chain, then began lecturing. Ricky might have laughed, but her tone was dead serious.

"You leave Elmer alone. He has a right to be outside. I don't want you frightening him. All of you, let him be." She pulled her hat off and thrust it at Ricky. "Rub it on your dog." He did as directed. She held the hat under the big dog's nose. "This is what Elmer smells like. He's a good dog. You are not to bother him anymore." For a moment her voice lost its flatness.

"Now, bring him closer." Ricky tried to reel Elmer in but had to pick him up again. He set him down about five feet from the fence.

"This is Elmer," she said to her dogs. "Let him be."

Elmer whimpered and looked cagey, as if he were on stage. He wagged his tail feebly to show he meant no harm.

"Oh, thank you so much! Oh, I'm sure this will help. I can't thank you enough."

The red-gold dog came close and wagged her tail. Ricky started to put his hand through one of the holes to pet her.

"Don't," said his neighbor. Her voice had gone flat again.

"All right, if you don't think . . ." He asked how long she had lived in Brighton Green.

She gave him a hostile, puzzled glance, as if he had asked a very personal question but decided to answer. "Twenty-two years."

"You must take in strays."

"You can't let them starve."

"Are they all fixed, if you don't mind my asking?"

"What?"

"Neutered. Are they neutered?"

"Yes." Again the mistrustful look. "They go to the Humane Society for that," she said as if reciting. "They neuter them for forty dollars. I can't afford it. But what else can I do?"

"Nothing," he said. She might be a bit nuts all right, but he had to admire her skill with the black dog. Yet, except for him, the dogs looked only halfway cared for. The fuzzy gray one's fur was matted; the little heavyset brown one had a patch of rashy skin it kept scratching.

"People would let them starve," she continued in a complaining voice. "They dump them. Why won't people do what they should when all dogs do is look to us? They look to us!" Her eyes reminded him of crazy people on television who were in a fury over some personal injustice.

"I know," he said. "It's bad."

"It's more than that. It's cruel. That's what it is. Cruel." She hugged herself as if trying to warm herself against other people's cruelty.

"I guess it is." How weak his voice sounded. Later, he felt the need to discuss the nature of this woman's illness with someone. Very likely she suffered from more than depression.

He called Betty. "Can I come down later and gossip awhile?"

When he arrived that evening after supper, she asked if he wanted decaf or regular? "I shouldn't do regular, but I love it so. Let's be really decadent and have chocolate cake too."

"What an angel you are, Betty!"

She led him into her family room with its big stone fireplace where she had made a fire just for him since the temperature had dropped. He sat down in an easy chair and put his feet on the hearth. Betty went into the kitchen and returned with a tray holding a stainless steel coffee decanter, two white cups, and two generous slices of cake on orange ceramic plates.

She set his plate before him and sank into another chair. Together they sat staring at the flames, sipping their coffee. In the firelight, he saw her eyes gleam. Her skin, quite pretty skin actually, had taken on a pinkish-orange tinge from the fire. Out of the corner of his eye, he watched her large bosom rise and fall.

He relayed the encounter with his neighbor.

"Well, maybe you can get through to her. Michelle and Lance keep saying they're going to call the authorities. She isn't coming to Brightonfest, is she?"

"I don't know. We didn't talk about it."

"She'd be like a fish out of water." Betty shook her head. "There's no way she'll come. She never has before. Why would she?"

"Do *you* think she's totally crazy?" He ate a bite of cake.

Betty scratched her throat with one of the end pieces of her glasses. "Yes. Don't you?" She turned to Ricky, smiling a motherly smile. "Someone who wants to be alone all the time. Not to want to be around people at all . . . But I am reminded of Calvin Coolidge: 'Any man who doesn't like dogs doesn't deserve to be in the White House.'"

The fire flickered and crackled. A chunk of log fell with a hiss. Betty poured more coffee. They gossiped about Cecilia and the Griffins, then talked on in a self-congratulatory way of why some people, people like themselves, loved dogs so much and other people disdained them. Ricky felt a dull contentment fill his body.

"Some people don't like that doggy smell," Betty said. "I love it."

"Their devotion. Their adoring eyes," he murmured. He had relaxed into a state of bliss. He felt he could say anything to Betty. But what to say? They fell silent.

"I don't know why I concern myself with her," he muttered. "Maybe it's her eyes. She has a dog's eyes. Dogs always look as if they're suffering or on the verge of suffering." It seemed to Ricky he had hit on something very insightful.

Betty stirred, sat up in her chair. "You're being silly. Have some more cake."

⟷

Brightonfest: Eighteenth Annual Celebration of Brighton Green Neighborhood the flyer read. *Calling every Hans and Heidi. Drag out your lederhosen, your dirndl skirts. Braid your hair. Don your alpine caps. Enjoy brats, burgers, German potato salad, kraut, and our special German pastries. This coming Saturday, 1 p.m. 'til? Shelter house on the green.*

To prove his good sportsmanship, Ricky put out forty dollars to rent a *Complete Alpine Outfit (Male)* consisting of brown lederhosen, green suspenders trimmed in braid, a long-sleeved white shirt, white stockings, alpine hat, and boots. Carrying his homemade streusel, he showed up early to help set up the tables. A couple of teenage boys poked each other and grinned at him, and a boy in a ragged T-shirt with *Bad Asp* imprinted yodeled. Teenagers set up a volleyball net and got a game going. Smaller kids ran around the periphery screaming. A sulky, thin, pimply-faced boy of around thirteen in a scarlet vest carried a wooden stool to a corner of the shelter house and tugged a baby stroller bearing an accordion up the stairs, his mother following with a music stand. Soon, halting versions of "Edelweiss" and "Liechtensteiner Polka" made it impossible to relax.

Ricky was the only man in costume. Michelle had said, "Everyone gets into it, costumes, the whole bit." But the other men all wore short-sleeved knit shirts and jeans or chinos, though several had beer bellies that suggested they would be right at home in a beer garden. One man had brought his stein collection and now wrote each man's name on labels he had affixed. Lance arrived, looking more ministerial than usual with his newly shorn hair.

Several women did arrive in costume, notably Michelle and Betty. Betty, in her long print skirt, white apron, and waist cincher that barely cinched, had a little trouble getting up and down the shelter house steps. Michelle, who had come as a beer-hall waitress, wore a low-cut blouse with short, puffed sleeves. Her waist was held in with spandex, and the bodice was tightly laced. Underneath the short skirt was a stiff petticoat, and every now and then the guests were treated to a view of red satin shorts. "Christian counselor, my grandmother," Ricky muttered.

Ricky went around introducing himself. "Good job," he said to the accordionist, who, recognizing insincerity, glowered. Betty handed Ricky a paper plate holding a hamburger, a bratwurst, and a huge scoop of potato salad. They sat at long tables covered with red-and-white checked plastic tablecloths, decorated with ceramic pumpkins, black cats, and other knickknacks Cecilia had found at dollar stores. Someone had set up a keg, and the man with the stein collection handed Ricky a small stein shaped like a Franciscan monk.

Betty was occupied, so Ricky sat down next to the teenager in the *Bad Asp* shirt and introduced himself.

After the meal, Lance Griffin rose and stood at the end of one of the tables. "I hope you've all met Ricky Solis, if you haven't already," he said. "Too bad our new neighbors, the Clevingers, couldn't make it. Be sure and stop by and introduce yourselves."

Lance was a droning speaker with the annoying habit of clamping his lips together, then releasing them with a kissing sound. He listed all the problems the Brighton Greeners faced. A few neighbors ("You know who you are") were carting their trash to the curb far in advance of the trash truck. Others were failing to "lid" their trash, so trash was "fouling our beautiful neighborhood." Everyone was told to "take the necessary steps."

Lance thoughtfully smacked his lips again, and Michelle called out. "Don't forget the rocks!"

He struck his forehead. "Oh, the rocks, the rocks!"

"In your head," said the *Bad Asp* kid beneath his breath.

"Michelle's talking about those limestone rocks in the wall around the flagpole in the entryway," Lance said. "They're looking kind of whomp-sided. In all likelihood they got hit by a car."

Someone murmured "whomp-sided?" The boy next to Ricky laughed a sneering laugh.

Lance looked at him gravely. "Seriously, Chris, we should all want our neighborhood to be the best it can. Brighton Green is a neighborhood to be proud of. We're all very fortunate to live here where . . . we have diversity. We have . . . pride." Lance looked off into space. "Why, I wouldn't trade it for . . . Paris, France."

"Would you trade it for Paris, Texas?" the boy said softly.

"Lance! The wall!" Michelle shouted.

"Okay, okay. Hey now, we need some guys with strong backs to rebuild the wall. And I'm thinking a fence around it might not be a bad idea."

"A fence around a wall?" Ricky asked.

Lance faced Ricky, frowning. "Don't worry. It'll be inconspicuous."

"Aren't we going to discuss the dog woman down the street?" Cecilia called out.

"She's got a hell of a lot of dogs, doesn't she?" a young woman in a ball cap and wrap-around sunglasses asked. "Why don't we just call animal control?"

"Maybe Ricky would know how many," said Michelle. "Didn't you go over and try to make friends?"

He caught a few murmurs of surprise and some unfriendly looks. "I just took her a few tomatoes," he said. "Yes, she has several. They seem to be under control though." Everyone seemed to be frowning at him. Was it the lederhosen? To try to make them like him a little, he went into a comedy act, dramatizing Elmer's refusal to enter his own back yard. "Cecilia knows what a coward Elmer is, don't you?"

Let everyone despise him, despise his dog. Just so they didn't see him as a threat. "I thought I'd better do something. So I talk to her. Actually, she's kinda helpful. She comes out with a choke chain, puts it on that big black dog, yanks him back from my poor dog, who is climbing up my face . . ." He glimpsed a few smiles. "I mean, she tried her best to help me."

Lance Griffin folded his arms. "Well, did you get a count?"

"Count?"

"Of her dogs. Did you count them?"

"Oh, four or five."

"I thought she had seven," said the woman in the ball cap. "I thought someone said that. They say her yard smells to high heaven." She glared at Ricky. "Is that true?"

"Sometimes there's a little odor. She has trouble getting around. Maybe she has arthritis."

"I feel for her," said Michelle, "but I'd sure hate to live next to her. But this is a picnic. Let's not go there."

"No," said Lance. "We shouldn't dwell on people's shortcomings. The purpose of this get-together is togetherness."

"Well, where is *she*?" said Cecilia.

"We need a committee," said Lance.

"What's so fuckin' bad about dogs?" Chris said.

The upshot of all the dog-lady talk, which Ricky heard percolating in little conversations even after *action was taken*, was that he was now on a committee of two dog-friendly people, Betty and himself; two anti-dog people, or, as Lance said, "people who may have a negative attitude toward dogs," Michelle and Cecilia; and a dog-neutral person, a man familiar with city rules and regs, who was not present at the picnic because he was out of town. They might meet next week on neutral turf at this man's house.

Ricky left the picnic thinking he should warn his neighbor of what was afoot, maybe hint that she should try to improve her place, green it up a bit, but what could she do now? It was almost too late to plant grass seed.

But why alarm her? And Betty told him he shouldn't worry so much. "The Brighton Greeners aren't really so bad. Something will work out."

Ricky wasn't so sure. "I should have said something at the picnic," he told her. "I don't believe in barging into people's lives." He glanced at Betty. "I should have spoken up."

He was again in Betty's family room, after a dinner of fried catfish. And now they were eating an apple crumb cake he said was in a class of its own.

She shook her head as she refilled his coffee cup. "Don't worry. I've been over the limit several times. No one's ever turned me in."

Elmer had fallen in love with the dog next door, the one with yellow eyes, the female named Sally, who had a sweet face and bushy white tail, which might have been beautiful had it not been full of stickers, little clods of dirt, probably even shit.

Perhaps it was the chow in her calling to the chow in him. Close up, Ricky had seen that she too had a mottled purple tongue. Since his neighbor's help with the big, black dog, it had quit charging the fence and now lay watching Elmer like a jealous husband. The sweet-faced, reddish-gold bitch flirted with Elmer from afar, running up to the fence and bowing playfully, but he would not go near the fence because of the black dog, though he would run in closer, then tear madly around the yard, showing off.

"You like that strawberry blonde, don't you?" he teased Elmer, who would turn his warm brown eyes on him, cock his head to the side, and seem to say yes, indeed, he liked her very much.

"She's a loose one, that girl!" Ricky thought her the most attractive because she was the most sociable. The black dog was by far the healthiest, most magnificent specimen, but such a grave, solemn dog. The pretty female seemed, in spite of her surroundings, light of heart.

One cool Saturday morning he saw his neighbor outside, wearing an old, shapeless olive-green jacket. She walked slowly around the yard, bending over to rake dog waste into a sack. For a moment he thought of talking to her as if she were a normal person, maybe speaking frankly of the committee. A few days ago they *had* had a fairly ordinary conversation about the weather. It had turned quite warm before the rain came through and cooled the air a good twenty degrees or so. He had called *hello* to her and said, "It's really Indian summer," and she had said, "I don't like it. It's bad for the dogs. It sends the wrong signal."

"About the weather?"

"I don't like it," she repeated.

The conversation stopped there. That night he had a dream of the two dogs playing together and awoke with a strange little verse in his head, which repeated itself all day: "Chow calls to chow. Brown calls to brown."

<hr />

The dog-neutral person was Oscar Jackson, a black man around sixty, who, Betty said, had been a city commissioner and was now a consultant. Betty explained his job in detail— something abstruse and complicated about gas companies. "Oscar still knows city hall like the back of his hand," she said.

Oscar was a tall, elegantly dressed man. At the meeting he wore dark jeans and a handsome heather cashmere sweater. The Jacksons' dining room, wherein they met, was done in white and two shades of blue and accented with lots of silver pieces. In the center of the table was a shiny silver bowl with green and blue glass grapes, and above their heads loomed a silver and crystal chandelier.

Oscar had prepared for the meeting by making copies of the rules pertaining to pets within the city limits and had highlighted the sentence, "Each household restricted to three dogs or cats and may not exceed a total of five pets."

Michelle and Cecilia were already there though Ricky had arrived early. On seeing him, Michelle smiled, but her eyes looked foxy. "How *are* you, Ricky? I adored your strudel. But you called it *streusel.* Much more authentic."

Oscar got the meeting started by saying theirs was a *serious undertaking.* Then without a word he rose from the table, left them a moment, and carried in a silver tray loaded with orange pumpkin-shaped cookies, though he offered nothing to drink. "Almost forgot," he said, thrusting the tray at Ricky.

"A rule's a rule," Michelle said. "I'm for reporting her."

"I thought we were here to discuss," Ricky said. Why had he ever let himself be drafted? He felt a pain in his gut, as if he had overeaten.

"Yes," said Betty. "If she has four or five dogs, what's the harm? Can't we bend the rules a bit. I actually had five cats once upon a time *and* Heidi."

"Oh, Betty," said Michelle, "those were just stray kittens, and you found homes for most of them, thank God." Michelle slapped Betty on the wrist.

"I'm hopeless," Betty said.

"*Her* dogs were strays," Ricky said, trying to smile. "You have to admit she's trying to do something very kind."

Cecilia looked down at the pink-and-green crocheted afghan square she was working on.

"Not to her neighbors," she said angrily. "That big black one is scary."

"But she's got him under control. He's not even very territorial anymore. Everyone's dog gets out now and then," Ricky said.

"Would you say there are five?" Michelle eyed him closely.

"I think so."

Oscar folded his hands on the table. "In my opinion, we must make a home visit. I believe Ricky and Betty are the ones to go since they've shown themselves to be sympathetic. The rest of us would only alienate her."

"She doesn't care much for me," Betty said. "Once she slammed the door in my face."

"Maybe so," said Oscar in his deep voice. "But you're the best suited. The rest of you agree?" He passed the plate with the pumpkin cookies again, and Ricky took one, feeling silly. In fact, they all looked rather foolish, as if they had come for a trick-or-treat handout. He wished Betty had kept quiet about his neighbor's rudeness.

Every two weeks a navy SUV pulled up to her house, usually on Saturdays, and the man said to be her nephew got out. He was in his late thirties or early forties, thickly built, and often dressed in Kansas City Chiefs clothing. His neighbor would come outside and unlock the garage door; the nephew would haul in groceries and other supplies including several big sacks of dog food. Once or twice Ricky had seen the man and his neighbor talking in the driveway; that is, he talked while she stood somewhere nearby. Ricky sometimes caught a few phrases: *take it easy*, *gonna get cold*, *gotta be going*, and once, *Aunt Gail*.

In late October Ricky was outside raking when the nephew pulled up again. When he opened the back door to his SUV to unload the dog food, Ricky walked over and grabbed a sack.

"Thanks," said the man without pausing his work. He had his aunt's pear-shaped face but was fairer, with light brown hair, small, wide-set hazel eyes, and a reddish face. He seemed a get-down-to-business sort.

"How's your aunt doing? I'm Ricky Solis, by the way."

The nephew extended his hand. "Jason Molthen."

"Is she on your mother's side?"

"Sorry?"

"Ms. Hoag. She's your mother's sister?"

"Actually she's my mother's cousin. But I call her *Aunt Gail*."

"Everyone thinks you're her nephew."

Jason shrugged. "Everyone thinks wrong."

"What do you do, Jason?"

"Sell sporting goods—mainly water sports."

Ricky set the bag beside the garage door. Inside, the black dog's nose moved the blinds. "Is she doing all right?"

"Aunt Gail? Not really. What can I say? If you've been around her, you know she's not all there." He shrugged again. Ricky started to ask what was wrong with her, but Jason was knocking, and the door was opening.

"Nice to meet you, Ricky. Hey, Aunt Gail. How's it going?"

"Oh, all right," came the low voice. She stuck her head out the door and stared at Ricky.

"Just lending a bit of a hand."

Daylight savings stole an hour of evening light. Ricky had overbought on Halloween candy and found himself on the sofa watching television and eating candy bars, even feeding bites to Elmer. He and his dog were growing fat.

A cold, persistent rain came through, turning his neighbor's yard to muck again. The dogs' fur just above their bellies was coated, like stiffened paintbrush bristles.

Every now and then he would hear a howl or wail. The little Brittany shivered at the back door. The sweet-faced, reddish-gold dog looked as if she had been flocked with mud. His neighbor often met the dogs at the back door with an old towel and tried to wipe them off before they entered the house, but even at a distance he could tell she wasn't succeeding.

He lay awake thinking of things he might do to better the situation before he and Betty made the visit he dreaded. At the meeting he had consented to going with Betty, but he needed to put things off awhile. He had several weddings to attend to. Betty called him several times about the visit, though it was always on his mind.

"I'll be the bad cop, and you'll be the good, and it'll work out," she said.

"I don't know. I should never have agreed."

"But something has to be done?"

He wanted to ask *Why?* but said only, "I don't know."

"Come on over. I made the best apple cobbler I've ever made. Almost as good as your streusel."

He went but did not linger at her fireplace as in the past. Nor did he relay his conversation with Jason.

The past week he had been going to a garden center every day after work, each time buying a single bale of straw since only one fit in his trunk. The first afternoon he had done this he had gone to his neighbor's house and knocked timidly. "I hope you don't mind," he said, "but I bought something for your dogs." He glanced away. He was tired of her down-turned face, that sense of gloom and doom she carried with her always.

"What is it?"

"Some straw. I just noticed the dogs were getting so muddy."

"All the rain."

"Let me spread it around for you."

"Just put it over the fence." Then, after a long pause, she said in a voice flat and perfunctory, "Thank you."

"I'll help," he insisted. He carried his kitchen step stool to the back yard and used it to climb gingerly over the fence. Together they spread the straw over the muddiest areas. One of the dogs had dug a big hole.

"Oh my," he said.

"I'll take care of it."

"Let me. Do you have a shovel?"

"It's too muddy. Wait awhile."

"All right. Sure." He smiled. "We'll get 'er done."

"I don't know," she said, but for a moment it seemed her voice lost its flatness, and he took heart.

Sometimes he worked alone outside distributing the straw, and sometimes he worked with her though they said almost nothing. One day the two of them went around with plastic bags and removed the biggest part of the waste, which he double-bagged and carted off to a dumpster on his way to work. Another day they were working near each other, coat free since the weather was nice, and Ricky felt confident enough to speak more freely. "I have to tell you, Gail—you don't mind if I call you *Gail*, do you?—I hate to say this, but the neighbors have been complaining about your dogs. They don't bother me, but some of them are talking about calling animal control."

She was stooped over, raking the stuff into a bag. Now she stood up, let the rake drop. "Did they talk about me at that picnic? Bastards! They can't leave a person alone. They spy on me. I know they do." She spoke in a loud, shrill tone. "Tell them to leave my dogs alone."

He was surprised at the quickness of her anger and how suddenly her face had grown wooden. "I think everything will work out," he said soothingly. "But between us, you just need to work with them a little." And now he was Ricky, the PR guy. "Tell them you'll do what they want. Promise 'em the moon." He grinned, but she didn't smile back.

"At least say you're going to find a home for one or two. Say you've got someone in mind. Just tell them what they want to hear."

"Who would take them? You can't trust people. They dump them. Bastards. Bitches."

"Well," he said. "All right. We'll do our best."

He spent nearly two hundred dollars on a huge doghouse, a big, gray plastic thing. Maybe two or three of the dogs could share it, and if that worked out, he might buy her another.

She said nothing, in spite of its obvious cost. "Maybe she thinks it fell from heaven," he muttered, but his mood softened, and he took over an old army blanket to put inside. She caught him outside one afternoon as he raked leaves in front. "I can't pay you for that doghouse," she said. "I brought back your blanket. It'll only get wet. It's by your rose of Sharon. I used the straw."

"Okay. Why don't you get your helper to bring you more straw from time to time?"

"Oh, Jason. He's not concerned about me."

"I mean he brings the other things. Why would he mind?"

"He just would," she said sullenly.

"All right then. I'll bring you some now and then when you need it." But some responsibility on her part was called for. "Just let me know." He found his silly *Totally Weddings* business card with his office and cell numbers on it and handed it to her. "By the way, Betty Wilson and I would like to come over to discuss the dogs. I told you other people were complaining. I got put on a committee, but I went along because I'm pro-dog." He looked at her but saw not the slightest warming. "Betty's pro-dog too. That's why they picked us."

"I know *her*. She's a bitch. I don't trust her."

"She wants to help," Ricky said. "She loves dogs."

It made him mad to have to defend Betty, who was a good person, not like the others.

"Anyway, in the meantime, you probably ought to . . . you know, get ready for us. I know it's hard," he said, glancing sideways. "Do your best. We'd like to come Saturday in the afternoon—about three, if that's all right."

Her face looked muddled at first, then turned cold and ugly. "It's no one's damned business how I live."

"Look," he said, "I don't want them to take your pets, for God's sake. I'll see you Saturday." Later, looking out his window, he saw her call to the dogs, who came to huddle near her and watched her pull dog treats from her pocket to feed them. "I'm an idiot," he said aloud. But hadn't he tried to be friends, tried to warn her? What else could he do? That night when he looked out, he saw the big black dog lying on the straw next to the plastic doghouse, which shone in the moonlight like a huge cube of ice.

On Friday before he left for work, he watched her using a broom to sweep up a thick blanket of leaves in front of her house. "Couldn't you use a rake maybe? Like a normal person?" he thought to himself.

There were still days of brilliant blue sky, jewel-like against the increasingly somber weather. Leaves drifted down unceasingly, mercifully covering the soggy straw and new piles of dog poop next door. Ricky was glad he didn't have to see his work undone.

He pulled up and bagged his long-spent tomato and pepper plants, relieved not to have to deal with a garden anymore. There *was* something to be said for letting things come to an end.

Before the visit, Betty called to say she wanted to come half an hour early to "put our heads together." She arrived with a copy of the city ordinance to hand to Gail Hoag. "I plan to say the committee is prepared to compromise if she'll work with us. Who am I to throw stones?"

This sounded hopeful. "Oh Schatzi!" He nudged her elbow. "You who have exceeded the cat limit. Did you talk to Michelle?"

"Yes, but she's impossible. She wants us to ask her to get her yard sodded."

She had brought him a greasy sack full of peanut-butter cookies. Ricky quickly made them each a cup of hot tea in his microwave. They sat at his red Formica table in the kitchen, one of the few bright spots in the house.

"This spring I'm redecorating," he said. "I'm going back to white walls. Except I do like this knotty pine."

"It's classic." Betty looked around the kitchen at all his photographs. When he had first moved in, he had decided to keep everything simple, but later he'd compromised and hung some of his favorite photos: his daughter at age ten on her bicycle; his ex-wife, holding their infant son to her breast, though the breast itself was obscured; old friends from high school and college; his parents; Mike, who had loved and departed, raising a lop-sided coffee cup he had made in ceramics class.

He nodded towards Mike's picture. "Prime cause of my divorce."

The picture seemed to have taken the starch out of her. He might have confided a bit, but she became all business. "Listen," she said, "Michelle and Cecilia keep mentioning filing a complaint. Even Oscar, to tell you the truth." She looked away, and it became clear to him that a decision had been reached without him.

"What's the point in our going?" he said sharply.

"Well, I mean . . . it isn't a certainty. If she'll work with us."

"If we bring up a complaint, she'll go bananas. She won't trust me again. I don't think she does anyway." He almost said, "She doesn't trust you at all."

Elmer whined and drew closer. Ricky scratched him behind the ears. "She can't lose her dogs, Betty. That's all she has. I should have said that at Oscar's."

He rose to fetch an old corduroy jacket so worn he had thought of giving it to Goodwill. It looked like something his neighbor would wear. "Well, let's go then. She's probably waiting."

Once they were on his neighbor's porch, he heard the familiar yipping and yapping and a long, low howl, like a loud sigh. Gail Hoag opened the door to admit them but stood for a moment blankly in the doorway. At least she was wearing a clean shirt, a mannish-looking blue thing. Her tan trousers seemed to have been washed but were wrinkled, still showing stains. Her hair too looked clean and was in its usual ponytail, but she wore no makeup, and the circles beneath her eyes in the gray, afternoon light made her face look cadaverous. And there was a bad smell coming from the house, a pungent ammonia smell. "Should we sit out here on your porch?" he said quickly. She didn't move from the doorway. "Do you want to sit outside, Gail?"

Betty, evidently having steeled herself, said, "Oh, it's so nippy. Let's go in."

His neighbor moved aside without a word. Betty led the way inside. The living room seemed not so bad as he had expected, nor was that part of the dining room he could see in the dim light. He took a seat on the sofa next to a tall stack of newspapers.

He heard scratching at the back door. When his neighbor left to open the door, Betty put a hand to her chest and gave a little exhalation of disgust. The black dog was let in, followed by the red-gold bitch, the Brittany, and the two smaller dogs. Then a bedroom door opened to his right, and a dog he had never seen before entered, an old, short-haired, brindle-colored dog, who approached awkwardly to sniff Ricky's trouser leg and lie down on an odd rectangular piece of carpet in some dark color.

Six. She had six! And was there a seventh? He glimpsed something pinkish and piglike beneath the bed.

And, as his eyes grew more accustomed to the dimness, he saw his first impression of her house had been much too optimistic. Clearly she *had* made some kind of effort. The floor had been swept—you could see the track of the broom— but a film remained over everything. The low table in front of the old sofa had been wiped, but spots and congealed crud remained. Oh, the ugliness of it all. There was a huge stack of books in the corner from which emanated a moldy smell. He saw black (black!) cobwebs in the corners of the ceiling. On the floor was a drab green rug, tattering. One large oval area of the carpet and the floor adjacent to it appeared a slick black, probably from years of sprawling dogs. Through the kitchen door he saw a sack of trash spilling over with empty dog-food cans.

For a moment he was too shocked to speak. Fortunately, Betty began to talk, at first in a high, unnatural voice. "It's nice to visit with you, Gail," she said, and, without waiting for a response, explained why they had come ("just to sit and chat a spell"). Then, her voice becoming more natural, she explained the ordinance. "We need to focus on some concerns, not that any of us is a Martha Stewart or anything." He was grateful she had taken it upon herself to state the problem, but, if you looked at it from Gail Hoag's point of view, this visit must be detestable. He felt he must say something. Hadn't he tried, in his way, to be her friend?

"I'm sorry about this," he said. "We thought . . . Betty and I . . . that we could help. There are others . . . not so sympathetic."

Yet another dog entered from the bedroom, an old, long-haired, white thing with matted fur. Betty talked on a few minutes about how they had missed her at the picnic, becoming again an altogether different Betty, one who sounded like a church volunteer at a nursing home.

"I don't go to those things," Gail said, giving Betty a hard, disbelieving stare.

Betty ignored her. "I was thinking we just might contact Animal Haven. I bet they'd be glad to find homes for a few. I'm sure they'd work with us." The last of her sentence rose as if it were a question.

"You can't have any of them!"

"But someone will call the city if you don't do something. We're on your side," Betty said.

"Then tell them not to take my dogs. And leave me alone!" The *alone* lengthened into a wail, and one of the dogs, perhaps the red-gold bitch, took it up.

"They'd kill them." His neighbor began wringing her hands and moaning. "No, you can't, you can't." Ricky felt he had been hit in the chest. He rose and went toward her. "Gail, please calm down. We want to help you."

"Yes, please calm down," Betty said in an annoyed voice. "Exactly how many are there altogether?"

"Ten, just ten. Five are old." She recited in a high, fast, mechanical voice: "Bobby, Ned, Bert, Bitsy, Pansy, Henry, Jake, Sally, Billy, Winnie. They'll put my old ones to sleep. They will. They'll put them to sleep. They're too old. They won't let them live."

"Then, you need to find homes for some of them," said Ricky in his most soothing voice. "If you could find homes for just a few. I would try to help you. I could take . . . one." He thought of Sally. "It would be right next door. I'd give it a good home." He looked to Betty to see if she would offer, but she was quiet. "Maybe I could even keep two. We'd find something."

"Go away, go away!"

"Please, Mrs. Hoag . . . Gail," said Betty.

"Go away. Bastards! Bitches!" She reached beneath a small end table into a pile of junk and fished out the leash she had used to control the big black dog earlier in the fall. At the end of the leash was a heavy silver chain, about two feet long. "Go, go," she said, shaking the chain at them.

They hurried out the door, which locked behind them. The big black dog shoved the blinds aside and was pulled back.

Betty shuddered. "She's crazy. It was filthy in there. Disgusting. We've got to do something."

"Let's have a cup of tea and talk first."

"She's absolutely nuts. I want to go home and shower. I feel so sorry for those poor dogs. One kept scratching, like it has fleas—the little brown one. I don't see how anyone can own animals and be so negligent. And the house. It's not just the dogs. She's really a danger to herself, Ricky."

"If they take her dogs, I don't know what she'll do. Please, let's talk about this."

"All right. But I want to clean up first. That house probably should be condemned."

"Oh, come on, Betty. I'm sure it's structurally sound. What are you saying? You're naturally upset because it's so dirty. But she's doing okay, for her I mean."

"Ricky, you can't mean that. She just threatened us. She's very sick."

"Yes, yes, but I mean she's holding on—or she was."

She shook her head again. "Go home and take a shower."

Betty did not call him, nor did she pick up when he tried to reach her. After work, he went next door to try to talk to his neighbor, but she wouldn't answer the door. He kept looking out his window for her to appear in the backyard, but she stayed inside, as did the dogs. He imagined the eleven of them huddling together inside the filthy house. It was all horrible.

He tried again the next day before leaving for work and again when he arrived home. He knocked and listened at her front door for footsteps but heard none, nor did he see the big black dog nosing the shutter aside as he had previously. But he did hear a whimper and, he thought, a voice commanding "hush." It was useless.

For several nights now he had not been sleeping well. One night he awoke from a dream in which he had been one of a pack of dogs, one of the submissive ones, and larger, more dominant dogs had threatened him, tussling, biting his pants legs, baring fangs.

He got out of bed to get a book he had left on the coffee table in the living room, clad only in boxer shorts, chilled because he lowered his thermostat to sixty at night.

Moonlight shone on the wood floor in the hall outside the bathroom's open door. He went to the window, standing in his bathtub to peer out above the frosted glass panes in the bottom section. Outside, a nearly full moon shone into his neighbor's yard, and in that light, augmented by the street light, he saw dark shapes moving about, one large, and one somewhat smaller and lighter, the black dog and the reddish-gold, he thought, though now she was nearly as dark as the other dog except for the light underside of her tail. There were other, smaller shapes. It seemed as if there were more than the usual three smaller ones, but perhaps his eyes were deceiving him. It was hard to keep track. They ran here and there, pausing to sniff, then bolting, springing up at something, at each other, running back and forth to the porch steps. Dogs freed from a long day of confinement. Why, she must have been letting them out at night all along.

And he saw with a start that she herself was sitting on her back steps tossing something to them. She had a dark blanket or cape gathered about her, hooding her head, but he could see her face when she turned toward his house, the moonlight making it appear paler than it looked during the day, for though her face was sallow, it had a woodenness that seemed to give it an underlying brown quality. But now she seemed to have shed that.

Little by little the dogs ceased their play and came to sit at her feet. Even the two largest, the black and the red-gold came to lie down nearby. She petted now one, now another, as if she were some sort of regal or religious figure dispensing favors.

After awhile she gathered up her blanket and her brood and went back inside, and Ricky returned to his bed. He couldn't sleep though he forced himself to think of other things.

Once at work he forgot his neighbor, the whole mess, and plunged into the job he thought so silly. He spent hours on the phone arranging things for a huge wedding, contacting suppliers of glassware, silver, linens, flowers. He placed countless orders. The bride-to-be called to say she wanted antique white or ivory napkins and matching napkin rings, "not that garish bright white." He tried to find the napkin rings she wanted without success and finally managed to locate some in a pale butter color. Would she be amenable? "Oh, don't cave on me yet," she said. He began to call suppliers outside the region.

In the afternoon, just before four, he picked up the ringing phone. "Hello," said the deep voice on the other end. For a moment, he thought he had the bride's father. Then a tirade of words: *outside, come to get my dogs, killers, bitches and bastards, bitches and bastards.*

"Gail?"

She hung up on him.

It took him a good forty minutes to get home through traffic. When he arrived, he expected to see the animal-control people outside her house, but the street was quiet and dim except for the rustling leaves that filled the gutters and skittered in the street. He knocked on her door, but no answer, and he could hear nothing inside the dark house.

At home there was a phone message from Betty: "Ricky, come see me when you get this, would you?" Her voice was chipper, but there was a grave undertone.

He called to say he would be right down and walked quickly to her house. She was waiting at the open front door.

"Coffee?"

"Sure," he said. He followed her into the kitchen. She was pouring coffee with her back to him, and when she turned to face him, she had the dumbstruck look of someone surprised by a blow.

"What is it?"

"It's very bad, I'm afraid. They took her away in an ambulance."

"What?"

"The ambulance took her—Gail Hoag. "

"What happened?" He set down his coffee cup.

"She went berserk. I heard it from Cecilia. She was there when it happened, probably outside pruning something that didn't need pruning. You know how she is." Betty perked up a bit. "Poor Cecilia. I think she kind of relished it."

"Tell me what happened, Betty."

"The animal-control people came, but she wouldn't let them in. Cecilia said she didn't know what she said to them. To hear her tell it . . . Well, her words were, 'I bet she threatened them.'

But anyway, they called the police, and a car came. Cecilia said something about a warrant. The cops told her if she didn't let them in, they'd have to break down her door. So she opened it. You can't believe how excited Cecilia got telling me all this. I thought she'd have a heart attack."

She poured herself another shot of coffee. Her hand shook a little replacing the pot on the warmer. She turned back to him with eager eyes.

"So anyway, she came outside, but she was 'absolutely nuts.' Just quoting, mind you. Cecilia told me in present tense if I can remember it: 'She says, "I'm not giving them up," and she comes out with some kind of a knife, and they don't wait a minute but they use a stun gun on her, and she drops to the ground like a load of bricks.' "

"Oh, God." He stared at Betty's kitchen counter—all the clutter. *Why, Betty could fall apart,* he thought. *So could I. What's holding us back?*

"I knew something bad would happen. She called me at work. How did she . . . ? Oh, I gave her my card. That's how . . ."

"She wanted you to help her?"

"No. She cussed me out."

"Well, you did what you could. Anyway, she's all right, I guess. Cecilia saw her get to her feet. I went down to talk to her—Cecilia, I mean. She said the nephew came out and locked the house up."

"He's not her nephew," Ricky said. "He's her cousin's son."

"Whatever. Anyway, they took the dogs to the animal-control shelter."

"Jesus Christ, they'll kill them."

"Not necessarily, not if they can find a home."

"Oh, Betty, you know how that works. They won't find homes."

"Maybe some won't. There were a couple that were very sick. You saw. It's really for the best."

"My God, Betty. Look what we've done."

"Ricky, she's totally crazy. It's better this way. Maybe they can find homes for the ones that are adoptable."

He grabbed his jacket. "Betty, she had nice dogs." He sounded like a pitiful child. "There's a pretty one, very sweet. Elmer adores her. And the black one is magnificent really. A nice little Brittany . . . " He stopped at the door, not wanting to leave. What would he find at the animal shelter? "A stun gun!"

Back at his house, he called the shelter but was shunted to a machine where he left a message to please not put any of the dogs down, that the owner's friends were looking for homes. He left his number, identifying himself as a concerned neighbor.

Again he put on his coat and took his car keys, but as he was pulling out of his driveway, he caught sight of the SUV coming down the street. He pulled back into his driveway and waited.

Jason opened his door and slid out. Seeing Ricky, he waved and called out "How's it going?" Jason moved more slowly, as if he were half asleep, like someone at a funeral. Above their heads a cold breeze twisted the caramel-colored leaves, breaking them loose. The two men stared at the still house and uneasily at each other.

"She's in a mental ward," Jason said. "They took her in an ambulance to Truman Hospital. Damn it to hell. Probably have to board up her back door until I can get that lock fixed. I got some exterior plywood in back." He nodded toward the SUV.

"What about her dogs?"

"I told the shelter lady anyone wants to adopt 'em, fine with me. If not, that's okay too. Do what they think is best."

"You wouldn't care if I took one, then?"

"Hell no, take every last motherfucker if you want. If they're still there, foster, adopt, whatever. No way she'll be out in time."

"What will happen to her?" He thought of telling this man of his last sight of his Aunt Gail, of how she had been reduced to sneaking her dogs out at night.

"I don't know. Depends on how she does. My thinking is she'd be better in an institution. I can't keep on like this. It's a wonder she hasn't burned the house down by now, not that it would be a great loss. The house, I mean." He glanced uneasily at Ricky. "I mean I don't want harm to come to her. She can't help the way she is."

Ricky was admitted by a rheumy-eyed man in charcoal gray trousers and a paler gray work shirt. Inside a small office, a woman in the same uniform was talking on the phone. When he entered, she looked up, smiled coolly and said, "Mr. Solis?" He nodded. "Mr. Molthen said you might drop by."

He took a seat. She clasped her hands together on the desk, then told him that five of the dogs had already been put down, three with severe mange, one pit bull, and one because it had a large, intestinal tumor and was suffering.

"But I never saw a pit bull," he said.

"An old one. It was a mix. Still illegal. She don't have a leg to stand on."

She stared at something on her desk that looked like a list. "I'm wrong. We had to put down six. The big black one. He was a menace."

"Oh no. He wasn't a menace with *her*." He looked away as tears sprang to his eyes. The man said, "It's a shame, but you have to think of pedestrians and such as that."

"What about the others? Can't I see who's left. How long before they're put to sleep?"

"The rest have got two full days. Somebody might take that chow mix. She'd be a nice dog if she was cleaned up," the man said.

"I want her."

The man took him into the holding room. There were maybe sixty-odd dogs inside. At first their reverberating noise was unbearable. Everywhere dogs rushed their cages, yipping, barking, whimpering, and wagging their tails, begging. A little beige and white spaniel with huge dark eyes whimpered and pressed against the cage to be petted.

"Some people'll dump anything," the guard said.

After several minutes in the shelter Ricky spotted the Brittany, the little fluffy gray dog, the fat brown one, and Sally. She lay quietly in her cage and raised her eyes to him as he drew near. He reached through the bar to pat her, but her tail barely thumped.

The man turned to him and confided in a whisper. "She was a lot better when they brought her in. I think she knows about the black one. Listen, pal, if you want to save a dog, you'd take one of the others. They're not likely to get a home, if you ask me, but she might. She's a pretty thing."

"Can I take all four?"

"The limit is three. You don't already have a dog, do you?"

"No."

"Go back in and talk to Mrs. Bryant."

He promised the woman he had a friend who would take the little fuzzy gray one. Perhaps Betty would, but probably not. If he couldn't find an owner, he would pay someone to pretend to seek ownership, and Ricky would keep it. Maybe he could talk the kid who'd worn the *Bad Asp* T-shirt into being a collaborator. It occurred to him that things might get more difficult, and eventually he might need to move out of Brighton Green.

He left the little gray one yipping plaintively in its cage. "I'll be back," he said.

He loaded Sally, the Brittany, whom he thought might be Jake, and the brown one into his back seat. Though he tried to block off the space between the front seats with his briefcase, the Brittany scrambled over it into the front. Ricky had to push him away from the steering wheel. The brown dog began scratching its stomach fiercely.

At stoplights he turned around to check on Sally, who lay quietly on the back seat. He reached back to stroke her red-gold fur, and she gazed up at him accusingly with her light, melancholy eyes.

Miss Mauve and Miss Green

Willa watched the door that opened onto the hallway. Soon Susan Brassfield and her sophomore English students would enter the library through it so her students could do research on an assigned topic, *My Potential Career*. While Willa waited with her co-worker, Esther Teague, they critiqued last night's *Producers' Showcase* production of *Peter Pan* with Mary Martin. Willa thought Martin too old to play Peter, though she was certainly slim and lithe, and she was too feminine, in spite of the short haircut.

"I don't see why they didn't just find a young actor," Willa said. "I found it disconcerting."

"Oh, everyone loves Mary," Esther said. "They equate her with Peter." Esther was drinking tea as she filed library cards and did paperwork at her messy desk, with its tea-stained and smudged papers. Esther was certainly not the neatest person. And she'd let herself get quite heavy.

And here came the students stomping down the steps. They plopped their books and notebooks onto desks. "Spread out," said Susan. "You girls take that table," she said to three girls to Willa's left. Willa and Esther came out from behind the oak enclosure where their desks were located to help the students with their research.

Willa was leafing through a bound collection of *Life* magazines for articles on Babe Ruth for a boy when she heard one of the girls in the threesome whisper something about "veiny, old-lady hands." Turning, Willa saw a thin, dopey girl with frizzy hair pointing at her. The other two girls were covering their mouths to keep from laughing.

She gave all three a hard stare and went off to help someone else. Later, back at her desk, she rubbed hand cream in and pressed on the veins. It really didn't matter that her hands were not her best feature. She had a good mind and absolutely perfect posture. Anyway, the girls were only in an average-ability class. Still, she had come close to crying.

Seventh hour, Susan was back in the library, this time with her accelerated seniors including Jerry Jarboe, a good-looking boy, who frequently wore a powder-blue sweater, which brought out his eyes.

Jerry was cutting up. He leaned over Esther's desk and punched her little bell as he sang the lyrics to "The Ballad of Davy Crockett":

Born on a mountaintop in Tennessee
Greenest state in the land of the free
Raised in the woods, so he knew every treeeeeee . . .

At *tree*, he punched the bell several times.

"Oh, for heaven's sakes," Susan said screwing her face into a little frown. "Don't be so *juvenile*."

Then a nice thing happened that made up for the awful girl. As Susan continued to scold, the boy turned his head and winked at Willa as if they were co-conspirators. Later, Susan said Jerry was absolutely brilliant, very artistic, very gifted, so . . . *expressive!* "But he can be an awful pain in the neck. He finishes his work at lightning speed. And then he's *trou-ble!*"

Willa had an inspiration. "Maybe he could be our student assistant? We'd have to check with Mr. Bonney, of course."

Willa told Esther here was an opportunity to decorate the library for free. Or if Susan was wrong and the boy's work was not good enough, they could use him in any number of ways—shelf checker, book shelver, book gluer, and so on. But she hoped he was creative. The library was such a fusty place. It was as if one were in a deep wood, a wood of oak where the sunlight rarely penetrated.

Before Willa, Esther had gone it alone except for ineffectual part-time help from a pasty-faced woman named Mrs. Mallett. But thankfully the school administration was finally persuaded Esther needed real help, and Willa was brought in. When she first arrived at the Southside High branch, she felt as if she had entered a Dickensian world— with dusty books piled high on the counters and book carts, even in corners, and Esther herself, a Dickens eccentric—a kindly, toadlike woman, who seldom rose from her chair, but squinted up at people through rimless spectacles. It had taken months of reshelving, discarding, repairing, and cataloguing to set things somewhat right.

The first day Jerry began work as an assistant, Esther and Willa gave him a little tour—first of the preschool/primary area where years back Esther had placed three little red chairs and a little red-and-blue painted wood table along with a now-dusty red plastic tea set and several picture books, including Potter's *The Tale of Peter Rabbit*. "Oh, I'm crazy about all the bright colors," Jerry said.

In the upper elementary room, he pointed to a set of children's biographies. "What an orange shelf!" He held up an orange-covered biography of Clara Barton. "Oh, I thought she was so noble. And I loved Helen Keller. And look! Davy Crockett! I wanted to be just like him. I had a fake coonskin cap I just loved."

Yes, Jerry was very effusive, very delightful. Esther immediately took him under her wing as she did the little children. Though Willa found Esther irritating at times, she had to admit Esther was good with children. They loved her because she was so grandmotherly and approachable, not much taller than they. If a child misbehaved, she would turn her head slightly and narrow her gaze until the child stopped whatever he or she was doing. Then she would smile and clap her hands and say, "Much better, dear."

However, Esther's use of storybook language could be annoying. She must have developed the vocabulary some time ago when the library story hour was a fledgling and storytelling styles more old-fashioned. A villain was a *slippery, slithery little man*; a cottage, *teensy tiny*. The little girls in the audience were *lovely lasses*; the boys, *stalwart young men*.

When Willa was hired, Esther told her she preferred working with the little ones and that Willa's work would be with the adolescents.

"Are there no adult books in your library?" Willa had asked. Her mission, she decided, would be to introduce more quality literary books. She would open doors.

"Oh, of course," Esther answered. "We have some for the upperclassmen, and if they're not on reserve, the public may check them out. We have a Steinbeck or two. We have a few Hemingways. We did have something by Mr. Fitzgerald, but someone borrowed it and never returned it."

"And Faulkner?"

"We have short stories. The novels are a little too adult."

This was Kansas City, not New York, but even so, over the years Willa had gotten several rather earthy books added, thanks to an alliance with Susan. They persuaded Esther to add—*East of Eden*, *Tender Is the Night*, an unabridged *Adventures of Huckleberry Finn*, and a book that might conceivably cause difficulties, *The Catcher in the Rye* by J. D. Salinger. Esther agreed to everything, though she said the Salinger book would remain behind the desk. She proved more accommodating than expected, and Willa was glad to see Esther would listen to her. And Jerry Jarboe might also be an ally.

Susan hadn't exaggerated. The boy was brilliant. He went immediately to work on the little children's area. To the lonely little plastic tea set, he added a bright array of objects made of poster board. One was a pale green plate with chocolate-chip cookies of papier-mâché, the chips made from bits of gravel he painted a shiny dark brown. He'd worked on the project at home, so they were getting even more than they'd hoped for.

When the two women raved about the cookies, he said, "Oh, I'm a fanatic for chocolate-chip anything."

"They look so tempting," said Esther. "But let's hope the little ones don't bite into them and break their itty-bitty chompers."

"Uh oh," said Jerry. "I guess I'll unstick the chips and paint them on."

"That would be best, dear," said Esther. "And I'll bake you some real cookies for your trouble."

Willa complimented him on the plates—all differently colored, with different floral borders of roses, iris, peonies, pansies. Besides the cookies, they held ruby-red, emerald-green, lemon-yellow, and orange gumdrops; shiny red and black licorice; pastel Valentine hearts with mottos aimed at young library patrons: WE LUV 2 READ. BOOKS R FRIENDS.

He made red-and-white checked place mats to set under the plates. From the ceiling he hung ribbon streamers to which he attached oversized cutouts of apples, oranges, pears, and grapes.

Esther was always hugging him. She would say, "Oh, I really wish we had money in the budget to pay you."

"Don't worry. It's a marvelous experience," he said. "I want to attend art school after I graduate."

"Jerry dear, we'll give you sterling recommendations," Esther said.

The next week she gave him money for poster board and paint so he wouldn't have to plague his art teacher. He rapidly sketched and finished cartoon-style covers of several of the Caldecott winners. For *The Little House* he did the house in the lower right-hand corner, glancing timidly up at a group of looming, older, bigger houses with moustaches, beards, and, in one case, breasts, which Esther asked him to remove.

They began having tea parties. Esther kept a tin of cookies inside her desk, and Willa would put the tea kettle on the burner. Jerry picked up mugs for the three of them at a junk shop—a green jadite mug for Willa, "because of your last name, of course"; a floral with a mauve background for Esther, "because of that mauve blouse you like so much." His was an ironstone mug—"because it's so manly, like me"—he said, rolling his eyes. Neither Esther nor Willa knew quite how to respond to *that*. Esther finally said, "To each his own."

Sometime in early April, Willa noticed Jerry's dress had changed from the conventional (the powder-blue sweater) to the avant-garde (lots of black with maybe a touch of color—a green belt, a pair of blue socks). He started calling

them *Miss Mauve* and *Miss Green*. Actually, Esther wore a good
deal more navy, but Willa thought Jerry insightful. The
mauve was more representative. And Jerry had, consciously
or unconsciously, given Willa a youthful color. Of course,
Green was her actual name, but still.

Sometimes she felt she and Jerry were peers, and Esther
the odd person out. Esther was not quite ten years older
than Willa, but Willa had kept her trim figure and brown
hair—not natural anymore, of course—so she looked fifteen,
maybe even twenty, years younger.

She found herself agreeing with Jerry that the upper
elementary room should be more grown up. "Yes, indeed,"
she said. "Some of the girls are already wearing lipstick."

Jerry raised his eyebrows at that, as if he were a parent
and not a seventeen-year-old.

"But Jerry, we mustn't encourage them," Esther said.
"We must keep things in good taste." Jerry grinned and
knitted his eyebrows a little. For just a moment his grin
looked devilish, like those pictures of horned imps one
sometimes saw in cartoons.

Willa did not want to dampen the boy's enthusiasm. "I
think," she said, "if you keep it subtle, it will be fine. Esther
almost always comes around. But subtlety is the key."

"Greenie," he whispered, "we're cohorts in crime."

The two of them decided the orange room, as Jerry had
labeled it because of the biographies, should become an
activity room. Esther was wary. "I don't know. A library
should encourage concentration and study. Activity?"

They were in the midst of one of their teas, which Willa
had come to look forward to. Earlier it had been disrupted
when an odd blond boy, a pale, wiry boy Willa had never
paid attention to before, came into the library with a message
for Jerry from Susan. Jerry got up and left the women briefly

to talk to the boy. Jerry lowered his voice and laughed at something, and it seemed the boys were friends.

"Another spot of tea, if you please, Miss Mauve," said Jerry when he rejoined them. Often he pretended to be British, and sometimes Willa played along.

"And who might that lad have been?" she asked.

"Oh, that's Vernon. He's in my class. Odd chap."

"What did he want?" Esther said in flat, Midwestern speech.

"Oh," said Jerry. "He just stopped by to say my presence was requested in class before the end of the hour. Bother!"

Esther looked at her watch. "Maybe you should go back now."

"Not yet. I wish to devour another of your marvelous crumpets."

They all sat around Esther's desk, Esther's ample body molded into her revolving chair, her plump stockinged legs visible above the sturdy black shoes she always wore. Willa sat upright in one of the plain oak chairs she had taken from the reference/study area. Jerry, wearing another of his black ensembles, perched on a corner of Esther's desk. Willa thought he looked good in black but much more handsome in the powder-blue sweater.

He took out a spiral notebook to show them his sketches for the upper elementary room—a football player with his hand drawn back, ready to throw; a ballerina in a tutu, her right leg at a ninety-degree angle; a man with glasses and a white coat peering into a microscope. He pointed to the man and said, with just a hint of smugness, "Mental activity."

"These will be very good, Jerry," Esther said. "We can set up a little table with books on careers."

Jerry took her hand and kissed it. "Thank you, Miss Mauve. About the figures. Should we suspend them or prop

them up? I can make propped-up people, but they're likely
to get knocked over."

"Better suspend them," Willa said.

It was as if they were at work on a movie. Esther was the
head of the studio, Jerry, the artistic director. And she? She
was the producer or whoever it was that got things done.

Within a week, the football player, the ballerina, and
the scientist peopled the orange room. Jerry added a
bricklayer building a wall because Esther had said, "Someone
should represent labor." Then they all decided there should
be a businessman, so Jerry sketched a man in a business suit,
who was, he said, an accountant.

"But what can I have him doing besides working in a
ledger? I can't seem to come up with anything interesting."

"Oh, just make the ledger colorful," Esther said.

"I suppose you could have a wicked-looking letter
opener," Willa said.

They really could think of nothing very good. If Jerry
were to portray a librarian, there would be the same problem.
Would you show her shelving a book? Or peering over
someone's shoulder as she was now doing, as they puzzled
over the accountant?

After school, Jerry dropped by, as he often did when his
mother didn't need him at home. Sometimes a dark-haired,
bookish girl named Roberta came too. But today the odd
blond boy, Vernon, came with him and hung around,
thumbing through handouts on top of the card catalogue,
then spinning the globe, stopping it with his finger on . . .
it looked like . . . somewhere in Africa.

The boy was apparently the same age as Jerry, though in
some ways he looked younger because of his slight, pale body.
But in other ways he seemed older. He had narrow, deeply
recessed eyes and a large pink lower lip that made him seem

to be always pouting. Today he wore a short-sleeved shirt with the top partly unbuttoned and his undershirt exposed as well as some kind of gold chain and pendant. As he drew nearer and bent over the desk, the pendant fell out of his shirt and dangled in front of her.

"What is that?" she asked the boy. For some reason she found his presence extremely disconcerting.

"Cancer—the crab. My birth sign." He glanced down, ran a finger over the pendant, and gave her a wide grin that was half sneer.

Now he was leaning even farther over the desk, blocking her view of Jerry's sketches.

"Hey, Vern, how can we make the accountant more interesting?" Jerry asked.

"Put a damn monkey in his pocket."

Jerry burst out laughing. "A monkey! Bizarre! You're so weird, Vern."

Willa nearly gasped though Esther seemed barely to notice. What did Vernon mean? Was he referring to the monkey on your back heroin addicts spoke of? But Jerry seemed to think it funny, so she smiled and raised her eyebrows a little.

He looked at her thoughtfully. "Oh, he's only being silly."

The boys left the library soon after to meet Roberta, who waited outside. Seeing the three of them walk off together, Willa felt very old, so . . . left behind. This odd boy had interjected a note of mockery. Or something more.

The next day before Jerry set to work on the accountant, he said, "That Vern. Don't mind him. He's crazy." He was standing beside her, handing her the finished sketch of the accountant, awaiting her response.

"I love the pocket watch. You have such an eye for detail." Across the way, she saw the ballerina spinning, suspended by a thread. Jerry had made her blonde and pretty with a star-shaped beauty mark and a silvery-pink tutu. Yesterday, two little girls in uniforms from the local Catholic school had stared up at her, and one had said, "Look at her beautiful shoes." The shoes were a pale silvery pink, and somehow Jerry had made them look like satin.

Willa was sure one day Jerry would be a great artist. He would leave them all in the dust, a thought that made Willa both happy and sad, as a mother might feel about her brilliant offspring. As for the accountant, thank heavens there was no monkey but instead a whimsical purple handkerchief with red polka dots.

The biggest problem was the high school room. Even before Jerry, Willa and Esther agreed there was a certain spookiness about it. There was one little window on the east, but the light was blocked by a wall, and in the afternoon, the room became almost foreboding. A few bare bulbs cast light down onto the tall narrow stacks. Into this room were crammed all the books for adolescents and adults—an odd assortment. One might find Lloyd Douglass's *The Robe* next to Daphne du Maurier's *Rebecca*, Robert A. Heinlein's books next to works by Hemingway.

"It's like something out of Poe," Jerry said. "But with tomes instead of tombs." He gestured toward the classics shelf up high where dusty volumes of Whitman, Emerson, Thoreau, and Longfellow were lodged. Willa thought of that shelf as the forgotten shelf and had suggested to Esther that maybe they should ask to store the books in the basement at the main branch.

"Oh no, Willa dear, that shelf is for the *patrons*," Esther said, crinkling up her eyes. "If there's ever any difficulty about what we do here, I point to that shelf."

"About the pictures. Maybe we should use images from Poe's stories," Jerry said. "We could do the black cat, the pendulum, maybe a house with a cracked wall." He had an eager look, as if he were about to bite into something. "Teenagers would go for it."

"Oh, I know young people can be full of Sturm und Drang, but let's not encourage it. Besides, how would figures from Poe alleviate the darkness?" Esther said.

Jerry frowned. "All right," he said, sighing. "I guess I'll have to come up with something else."

"Oh, you'll think of something wonderful," said Willa. "And when you get everything done, we ought to have a little open house to celebrate the library's new look. You could invite your English class." Of course, that meant the strange boy would be invited too, but she could put up with it.

"Oh yes, Jerry," said Esther. "You've worked wonders."

Jerry touched the top of his head, then his heart, and then bowed. "Miss Mauve, Miss Green—ladies. I salute you." He clicked his heels together.

While Jerry deliberated about the mature-readers' room, he painted an assortment of flowers free-handed in the girls'/women's restroom and all kinds of hats and caps in the boys'/men's. When they were about to have tea, Willa would go fetch him and would find it discomfiting to have to go into the men's, to first knock carefully on the door and call out, to be told to enter, then walk in, feeling as if one were about to chance upon something unpleasant. There was such an echoing quality inside, one felt somehow disembodied.

Also, one would find oneself glancing, against one's will, past the wall that blocked the urinals from sight, and glimpse them, and though they were kept quite clean, so clean one was reminded of drinking fountains, that made it even worse.

Around the beginning of May, Jerry finished the bathrooms and drew a grapevine with curling tendrils around the entire reading/study room, painting in occasional bunches of grapes and the heads of famous writers—Shakespeare and the usual people, including two women, Jane Austen and Emily Brontë. Esther said, "Maybe there should be a Negro writer since the schools are now integrated." After consulting with Susan, Willa suggested Jerry attempt a portrait of Langston Hughes, and he completed a fairly good likeness, though Willa thought he made Hughes's features a little too pronounced.

Not long after, a man came to the library after school to pick up his daughter, a delicate girl with light brown skin, who sat quietly at a table working on a term paper. The father, however, was darker. He entered cap in hand and sat beside the girl, glancing around nervously as she finished copying something from *Life*. From time to time Willa noticed him staring at the faces on the wall, especially the portrait of Hughes. Then he leaned his head on his hands. Feeling a sudden sympathy for him, this man apparently beaten down by life, maybe a bit like herself, she had an impulse to help him.

Gathering her courage, she rose from her desk and made her way toward him. "How do you do?" she said to the man. "How are you, Lily?" The *Life* article, she saw, had to do with Hemingway and *The Old Man and the Sea*.

The father and daughter nodded.

"I noticed you were looking at the picture of Langston Hughes," she said, feeling a little silly. "We have his works if you're interested. Haven't you studied him in English, Lily?"

"Just 'Dream Deferred,'" said the girl, her mouth open a bit. "That's all."

"Have you read any of the stories about Jesse Semple, sir? They're absolutely marvelous."

"Can't say I have," said the man, staring up at her.

She brought him the book, but later when she glanced his way, she saw he was sitting with his head in his hands.

"I don't know where I'm going to put things in this room," Jerry said. "I can't hang things from the ceiling because the stacks are so narrow they'd be batting against the shelves. And there's no wall space to speak of."

"Oh," said Willa, "you'll think of something." The day was sunny, and the room seemed not so oppressive as usual. Her heart felt lighter. It's spring, she thought. It frees one. One should not be so ridiculous.

"Or," she said, feeling whimsical, "there's the floor." She thought of "The Face on the Barroom Floor" and the fuzzy image of a disembodied head of a woman painted on a floor somewhere in Utah or Colorado came to mind.

"The floor?"

The two of them looked down.

"It's an ugly floor," he said. "Someone's painted it a dark brown."

"It probably hasn't been cleaned well in years. Jerry," she said, touching him lightly on the arm, "why couldn't we give it a good scrubbing and then paint it a light color, something washable? It would be your background."

"Well, yes," he said. "But it would be quite a job."

This was true, and for a moment she had the feeling she and Esther were asking too much of the boy. After all, his only pay was in tea and cookies. But she could help. The idea of the two of them working as partners was gratifying. Today he was wearing the blue sweater she liked so much.

He walked up and down the aisles of the stacks, thinking.

"It will have to be sanded, won't it? I mean for the paint to take well."

"Yes," she said. "And I imagine we'd need some kind of sealer to protect your art. Well, what do you think? I give you free reign," she said impulsively. "Do what you want."

"I think you're a genius, Greenie." He shook her hand vigorously, then gave her a little kiss on the cheek. "Maybe I could get my friends to help."

"I don't know," she said. She really didn't want anyone else. "I wouldn't mind doing that sort of work."

"Oh," he said. "Well, sure."

"Come now," she said, leading him back towards Esther's desk. "Let's have tea."

She was very sorry to learn the next day that Jerry had enlisted his friends. "All right. But just for the hard labor," she said. "And I'll help too. So you can get to your art sooner."

"Actually Vernon's pretty good in art."

"I don't know," she said. "I thought perhaps I . . ."

"We want to finish it before I graduate, don't we? Now, Greenie"—he frowned at her in a pretense of sternness—"you shouldn't have to get down on your hands and knees."

Roberta soon flagged. Checking on how things were progressing, Willa caught sight of her sitting on a low stool looking through a Sherlock Holmes. "Oh, look," the girl said. "It's got 'The Red-Headed League.' "

"Yes," said Willa. "It's marvelous." She was torn between wanting to discuss the story (And, after all, it *was* her job to encourage reading.) and wanting to tell the girl to get back to work. But Roberta was a volunteer.

"Why don't you check it out later?" she said, smiling, glancing down at Roberta's bucket of soapy water. The girl took the hint and replaced the book, but not long after, when Willa had finished shelving books, she discovered Roberta had checked it out and left.

With Roberta gone, Willa insisted she would help the boys and the next day brought an old pair of blue jeans and shirt to work in. It was very hard work cleaning the floor, but not unpleasant because Vernon was working in a far-off aisle. She found his voice extremely annoying, crude, and suggestive. "Jerry, Jerry, Jerry," he would call out, and she would visualize Vernon raising his upper lip, like a horse snuffling over a carrot.

She forgot him awhile as she and Jerry discussed his college plans. "I don't want to do commercial art," he told her, "but I'll probably have to for a while. I wouldn't mind doing decoration though. Like we're doing. It's fun. And you don't have to work forever on it."

"Yes," she said. Of course, what he had done for the library *was* decoration, but she had thought of it as something more.

"Well, it's very good decoration—if that's what it is."

"Thank you, Greenie. Hey, I have an idea. Why don't we do the Greek gods? We could do Zeus and Poseidon and Hera and the whole bunch."

"Why, that would be wonderful."

Vernon had drawn closer. "Nah," he said, in a guttural voice. "Let's do something funny. How about Bugs Bunny, Jer? Jerry, Jerry, Jerry, how about Daffy Duck?" Vernon pushed his lips out. "Thath's dethpicable."

"You're dethpicable," said Jerry. "Get serious. Don't be a boob."

"What's up, Doc? I am a boob. I love boobs! Boobs are the opposite of dethpicable. Boobs are thtupendous!"

Jerry laughed. "You love boobs. I don't love boobs. You know that, doncha?"

Willa stared at him. She had never heard this kind of talk from him before, as if he had forgotten her altogether. Both boys' voices had coarsened.

"You're a boo-boo head, if you don't." Vernon said. They laughed loudly, making snorting sounds. Willa got to her feet, deciding it was time to distance herself. "Let's don't get too carried away," she said coldly. They stopped momentarily, but after she went back to work, the laughter began again.

"They're being childish in there," she told Esther. "They're getting on my nerves, especially that friend. He's very crude."

Esther was sitting at her desk, regluing the cover on one of the orange biographies. "I know what you mean. Teenagers can be bothersome."

"I don't like that boy."

"My sincere apologies, Greenie," Jerry said later. "Vern always gets me going. We were kind of Looney Tunes back there. Seriously, I was thinking of making the figures like El Greco's. They're going to have to be elongated anyway because of the narrow space. But that's all right because the gods were rather strange characters."

He began work on Zeus, sketching him first against the light-brown paint they had applied, then filling him in with long, white hair, a shield in his right hand, and a twisted oak tree in the other.

The next day Vernon, wearing an old work shirt with *Country Club Dairy* on it, got down on his hands and knees to work on Zeus's eagle. He knelt over the eagle, stippling its feathers, reminding her of a tattoo artist at work. Now and then noisy laughter would break out, and one day she caught Vernon standing at the opening to one of the stacks, with his left hand in his arm pit, pumping his right arm to make the sound of someone breaking wind.

She was infuriated. "We can't have that in the library!" she said. "Honestly, Vernon, you'll have to stop that right this minute."

Both boys looked at her as if they thought of her as a prudish librarian.

Fortunately, just as Jerry began work on Hera, Vernon was off for several days. When Willa asked Jerry where his friend was, he said, "I'm not sure. It's a skin problem—a rash or hives or something." He looked down at Hera. "I'm going to do her in gold, but other than that, I don't know. The main thing about old Hera is that she was always going after Zeus's girlfriends."

"I suppose. Isn't she associated with the peacock? Can you do a peacock?"

"Vern can when he gets back."

"I'm sure you can do it very well by yourself."

Jerry finished Hera quickly, as if he were uninspired by her. He made her gown gold with green trim and gave her an anxious, sour face. Vernon returned after three days, his arms encrusted with brown scabs—he'd had a staph infection. Willa could barely stand to look at him, and though she had to admit his peacock was well done, he had made it disproportionately large, its chest such a bright greenish blue it outshone Hera.

They then completed Athena and a fierce-looking owl, Mercury with winged sandals, and Poseidon with his trident. Willa thought she might as well stay out of their way and forced herself to work on typing new library cards and a list of new acquisitions for the teachers.

Over and over the sounds of crude, animal-like laughter came from the stacks. Or perhaps Vernon, who had begun to wear form-fitting, short-sleeved shirts now that it was warm, would appear with a dab of paint on his face. Once it looked as if someone had drawn a moustache.

She and Esther were now having their tea alone. How she missed the teas with Jerry before Vernon's appearance, the repartee they'd shared. But she did not offer tea to the boys because she felt Vernon would make fun.

One day she looked up to see Vernon shoving aside a chair as he headed her way. "I liked it better without him," she said to Esther.

"Is it okay if we do Cerberus?" The boy was grinning from ear to ear. "You know what kinda dog he was?"

"No, I don't," said Willa, trying to keep her composure. "I'll have to look it up."

"He's got three heads," said Vernon. "So I guess we could do three kindsa dogs." He rolled his head down onto his chest, then brought it back into position, giving them each a silly grin.

"I don't know about *that*," said Willa. "I think we should strive for some kind of authenticity."

"But," Esther said softly, smiling at Vernon in her grandmotherly sort of way, "I don't see that it matters much," she said. "Any kind will do." When Vernon had gone back to work, she said, "Remember, dear, you promised Jerry free reign. Anyway, what does it matter?"

"I need to keep an eye out," Willa said.

Esther frowned. "You seem a little overwrought."

At the end of the hour Jerry approached them, smiling. "Come and see, ladies."

Esther got up creakily and ambled over to the three-headed creature, Willa following. Well, it was all right. Though the animal was rather unsettling to look at, she had to say it was well-executed. Each of the dog's heads resembled the breed it was supposed to resemble. There was a bright-eyed cocker spaniel, a Doberman, and a boxer, all attached to a body that began in fur, which turned to scales and ended in a dragon's tail.

She had to admit Vernon also had a degree of talent. That disturbed her a little, perhaps because she had never had artistic talent. It was another way she had been slighted.

At home, in the bland rooms she rented, she found herself dwelling on how she'd been cheated by life. She *was* overwrought and should try to overcome this feeling. Perhaps she should take a day or two and drive somewhere, some place where she might see something, though where she would drive she couldn't say. She imagined traveling all the way to St. Louis and visiting the art museum. Then perhaps she might go into a small gallery and actually buy a work of art to bring home. "I should do something," she said.

On Sunday afternoon she called her younger, married sister, Ann, and asked her to see *Marty* starring Ernest Borgnine, but Ann's youngest daughter was ill, so Willa went alone. The movie had been advertised as a comedy, but she found it mostly sad since the main characters were both suffering, deserving loners and their moments of happiness so tentative. She sat through the film bundled up in her spring coat because, though it was May now, it was a chilly evening and the theater was cold.

Even work, which had been a solace, was becoming another thorn in her side because of the presence of Vernon. And she found Esther more and more irritating. Her eccentricities—the pencil stuck in her gray-brown hair, the narrow glasses attached to the beaded chain that rested on her large, mauve-covered bosom, the garish bunch of artificial violets she wore pinned to her coats, her habit of always making characters a "fuzzy wuzzy" or a "silly willy" or making cars (and trucks and tugboats) go "rootie, toot, toot" or making an insect's buzz invariably end in a t—all these things were harder and harder to bear.

She had not taken time off from work in quite a while, and now she felt she must, though she would possibly miss a private conversation with Jerry, and those conversations were so dear to her. And soon they would end. He would graduate May 25. She had imagined his return to the library years after he became a famous artist. "Miss Mauve and dear Miss Green," he might say, "you gave me my earliest canvasses."

Monday morning she phoned in sick. As she predicted, Esther called later to check on her.

"What is it? Tummy flu?"

"I'm just a little under the weather, that's all."

"It isn't . . . a woman thing is it? You've put all that silly willy stuff behind you, haven't you?"

"Oh no. Possibly I could have eaten something. I don't know."

"Well, take care, my dear."

Esther's voice was comforting, and as Willa lay on the couch, staring up at the ceiling most of the day, rising only to fix herself tea and toast as if she really *were* ill, she regretted any animosity towards Esther. But really, Willa ought to get away. Maybe she would drive south to see what the spring flowers were like where it was warmer. Perhaps she might be a bit depressed.

Tuesday she did drive south, but she got only forty miles or so out of town before it clouded up and began to rain. She pulled off to have a cup of tea and a sandwich in a little café, then decided she might as well head back.

⎯⎯◇⎯⎯

"There's been a lot of giggling in the stacks," said Esther when she returned. "They're doing Pan. Go take a look."

"But why Pan? He's a minor god."

"Because Vernon's forte is animals."

Willa had made up her mind to be pleasant. Hesitantly, she walked over to the dark room to see what the boys had created and found the half-goat, half-human figure of Pan in the last aisle. The figure was more tasteful than she had pictured. She had imagined a creature thoroughly hairy in the chest and nether regions the moment Esther had mentioned Pan, but though the hair and cloven feet were there, the creature looked more impish than lewd. He was bare chested with long brown locks and, oddly, delicate hands, troubling because of their twitchy-looking fingers.

"Miss Green, you're back," said Jerry as soon as the boys came into the library in the afternoon. "And not looking green at all. Say, I have a favor. I'm using you as one of my references in my application to KU."

She looked up to see if Vernon was listening to the conversation, but he had ambled away.

"I'd be pleased to write you a recommendation, Jerry,"
she said evenly. "I'll get started right away, and you can check
it before you leave to see if it's what you want."

"Thank you very much." He took her hand and kissed it.

The kiss was partly ironic, of course. But that did not
make it less delightful.

They seemed to have reached some kind of understanding.
He went off to put the finishing touches on Pan, and she
sat down to write, but her first draft was rather cramped and
tight, so weak and unhelpful she crumpled it up and tossed
it into the trash. "I must let things flow," she thought.

"This young man," she wrote, "excels in his ability to
adapt to circumstances as is often required of artists. He has
worked energetically and imaginatively to transform our
little branch library into a much more visually appealing
place. He has accomplished all this through excellent work
in a variety of artistic media. His paintings show amazing
mastery for someone his age. Patrons frequently compliment
his work." (Actually the only compliment had been from
the little girl who had commented on the ballet shoes, but
she felt she could allow one untruth.)

"I enthusiastically recommend him," she ended.

"Thank you, thank you," he said when she shyly handed
it to him. The entire hour she had felt shy around him. She
had barely spoken to him except to ask who might read the
application. Would it be for a committee? Someone in the
art department?

"They don't say. Don't worry. Whatever you write will
be fine," he had said as if he were consoling a child. And
yet after her extended weekend, she felt drained and old.
Like something cast off, something . . . without value. She
no longer felt herself. But perhaps—and the thought made
her wearier and sadder—she *was* herself.

Then she saw Vernon's face peering out of the men's restroom. He came toward her to brag about the figure of Pan. "Jerry does faces a lot better than I can. But I did the body."

"Well," she said, "that's good."

He shrugged, and she turned back to her work. Later when she was replacing books in the upper elementary room, she saw both boys disappear into the restroom. Not long after she heard Vernon's vulgar, snorting laughter and rose from her desk to take another look at the figure on the floor. Yes, someone had made the skin around the neck and chest as pale as Vernon's though down below, in the belly region, as the figure's goatishness became more evident, the figure became a hairy, ruddy brown. Of course, it was dark in the room due to the day's cloudiness, but it seemed to her that someone had sketched the figure's . . . well, it looked like the male organ. It was hard to tell because it had only been outlined faintly, and the outline was rather broken. Perhaps she was seeing things.

No, she looked again, and she was sure she was correct. Probably one or both boys had seen it as a joke, the soft broken line that would not be noticed at first but would be detected by the close observer. She felt her mouth drop open.

Of course, it must have been Jerry who had come up with the idea. It was too clever for Vernon, who would have made things crudely apparent. No, it was too subtle. What were the boys up to in the bathroom this very minute, she wondered. She paused to listen carefully. It seemed she could hear something like a long low chuckle escaping from within.

She stood there. Someone nudged her arm. Esther was standing beside her, handing her a cup of tea.

Ignatz

Howard's nephew needed a steward for a community garden. "It's in the urban core," Clark said. "All you need to do, Uncle Howard, is hang out and remind people to water. Maybe weed around the perimeter a little. Why don't you take a plot for yourself? There are three unclaimed ones under the blue tarps. If you could just put in two months to get things going, there's a little stipend."

His nephew was a community organizer—a good kid, but a doofus. It would be like him to try to organize a community, but you had to admire the nerve required since, in Howard's opinion, everything under the sun resisted organization, and, if things could be organized, they didn't remain so.

Obviously, Clark had picked him because he was available. But why not say yes? He used to like to garden, but now, in his tree-choked backyard, it was impossible.

It turned out *urban core* didn't necessarily mean slum. Some of the houses looked almost middle class, small and neat with hard-edged boxwood shrubs and white rock mulch, but others had old pickups and chain link in the front yard, and a passel of little kids. As Howard walked the garden's mulch pathways, a kid who looked like a gangbanger sauntered by with serious tats and underwear on display for all the world.

As for the garden, it had lots of early stuff—lettuce, onions, spinach, cabbage, radishes, cilantro. There were small tomato and pepper plants, many planted way too close. Clark knew fuck-all about gardening.

At the west end, a gravel alley sloped downhill to the north, like a dry creek bed. On both banks, itchy weeds stretched out long fingers to touch Howard as he checked out the terrain. He passed a garage leafed over with poison ivy, stared into a bare-dirt backyard with a bright turquoise above-ground pool filled with little kids, hollering and splashing.

Farther down, trees and shrubs formed a primitive colonnade with small openings into back yards. The alley sloped downhill for nearly a block but ended in a level area where big potholes overflowed from last night's rain. When Howard shaded his eyes, the pools merged into a single pool where blackbirds dunked and splattered themselves.

When he returned, a wiry old guy working his plot introduced himself as Dale Cutler. "This garden needs a sign telling people not to plant corn," Dale said. "Raccoon magnet. There's a pack comes down that alley every night." He pointed to a cage with an open door near a compost heap. "I get one or two a week and take 'em out in the country and let 'em go."

"I hear they starve to death when they're out of familiar territory," Howard said.

"Maybe they'll learn."

<hr />

His second day of stewardship, a skinny boy of nine or so stepped out of the alley to ask if he could plant *vejables*.

"Say what?" said Howard, playing the kid a little.

"Can I plant vejables here?"

"Pronounce your words, son."

"You know, like corn or tomatoes."

"A tomato's a fruit. Did you know that?"

"A *canalope's* a fruit."

"It's *cantaloupe* as in 'I want to elope with you, but I can't elope because I have to take out the garbage.'"

The boy looked annoyed. He wasn't a bad-looking kid with his wide-set eyes the light blue of an old mason jar, but he looked crafty. He wore cutoff jean shorts and no shirt and was turning red. Howard's daughter used to double coat her kids with sunscreen.

"What's that green thing?" the boy asked.

"A kohlrabi. Don't feel bad. Ninety percent of the population couldn't pick out the kohlrabi in a lineup."

"Whaddaya do with it?"

"What do you think? You eat it? I'm not crazy about it."

"How come?"

"It can't make up its mind. It wants to be a cabbage, but it doesn't have the heart. Get it?"

"Get what? Hey what's that thing over there with the big leaves?"

"That's rhubarb, young friend. Makes the best pie in the world."

"You put those leaves in a pie?"

"No way. If you ate the leaves, you'd fall over dead."

Across the street, a large woman on a porch shouted, "Hey there, Ennis! Get yourself on home!" She waved an arm in a limp circle.

"What kind of name is *Ennis*?"

"My dad's name. He lives in Oklahoma."

The boy headed home, returning ten minutes later with three more kids. "My family," he said—two girls, also fair and blue-eyed, and a small, dark-eyed boy of about six or seven. The skinny younger girl was ten and called *Shannon*; the older, pink-cheeked and well-endowed at twelve, was *Madison*. The little boy was *Ramón*. Ramón was a pretty-faced boy with black spiked hair and brighter eyes than the others, yet all four looked sly.

"This man—*Howard*'s his name—he's gonna let me plant stuff," Ennis said.

"I said *maybe*. I have to check with Clark. You all know Clark?"

"He's the guy wears cargo pants?" Shannon asked.

"No doubt. He's my nephew. I'm here as his lieutenant."

"You're in the army?" Madison said. "Aren't you too old?"

They all began shrieking about wanting their own garden, and Howard found himself the center of attention for the first time in ages.

"You can each have half a plot. Everyone pick two things, and I'll try to find them if Clark gives the go ahead."

Madison picked tomatoes and okra. Ennis picked cantaloupes and cherry tomatoes.

Shannon wanted the same. She looked as if Howard might slap her if she chose incorrectly.

"Just carrots," said Ramón.

"He's a half-brother. He's like a bunny rabbit," said Madison. "He loves carrots."

"That's why his eyes are so bright," Howard said.

"The family's pretty needy," Clark said when Howard called to update him. "It's a good thing you're doing, Uncle Howard. They won't forget this."

"Oh, kids forget all kinds of stuff. Good thing too. Otherwise, our minds would be full of crap." But Howard remembered his grandfather, who'd moved in with them, putting up strings for morning-glory vines and how painstakingly he had set screws into the side of the house and staked and tied strings in place. By late summer, vines had shaded the entire south side of the front porch and bloomed a beautiful blue, and every day, his grandfather called out "Morning, Glory" when Howard came down to breakfast.

At Lowe's he went crazy and bought eight kinds of tomatoes; five kinds of peppers, including serranos; bamboo poles for growing hyacinth bean vines to make a tepee; child-size gloves; and packages of cantaloupe, carrot, okra, sunflower, and popcorn seeds.

Afterwards, he met his buddy, Milt, for their monthly lunch at the Panera midway between their houses. They had been eating there because the food was healthier than pizza or burgers. Howard was tired of the Pick Two's, but Milt, who was cautious now that high cholesterol and acid reflux were part of the picture, was sure Panera would extend his life.

When he showed Milt the hodgepodge of stuff he'd bought, Milt sniffed and said, "Don't you know corn brings out raccoons?" Just like the old fart in the garden.

Howard told him about his new job and the kids he was working with, especially "this cute little kid named *Ignatz* or something."

For some reason Ignatz, the mouse character in the old Krazy Kat cartoons, had popped into his head. Howard's father used to call an ornery little neighbor kid *Ignatz*. That

Ignatz had a bit more going for him than this one and had grown up to become a lawyer, if something of a shyster.

He lugged all the stuff to the garden the next day and found the kids waiting, but after twenty minutes of sweating and digging in the dirt, Madison, Shannon, and Ramón put down their shovels and took off down the alley with Madison in the lead, like the cutout ducks an old lady had made to decorate the garden. She'd lined them up with beaks pointing north, like these kids, who turned their greedy faces towards Ramón's cousins' house, the one with the aboveground pool he'd passed his first day.

"Where are you all going?" Howard shouted.

"They got PlayStation," said Ramón.

"At least you're a true-blue gardener, Ignatz," Howard said when the others disappeared. Ennis frowned as if insulted.

"What's the matter? Ignatz was a mouse, kind of like Jerry in *Tom and Jerry*, but smarter. He was always lobbing bricks at Krazy Kat because Krazy drove him nuts."

The strip was hard to describe. Krazy loved Ignatz in spite of the mouse's hurling bricks, which the cat saw as missiles of love. "L'il dahlink," Krazy Kat would say. "L'il ainjil."

Howard and Ennis put up the bamboo tepee and planted the hyacinth beans near each pole. The next day Ennis brought over two signs to mark his family's plots: *Propity of the Hernandez and Jenkins Familys. Vilaters Will Be Prossecuted.* Every day when Howard drove up, Ennis came over to help him weed though his sisters and half-brother steered clear after figuring out no pay was involved. Sometimes he came from the cousins' house, where the kids stayed when their mother wasn't home. At first, Howard would mutter to himself as the boy approached, annoyed his thoughts were about to be disrupted. But what thoughts? Old gripes and gritches. Raggedy stuff.

The mother's name was Bethany Jenkins, he learned from the duck lady, who coincidentally was named *Helen Chick, Chick* being "the American version of *Chytka*," she told him. She was a tiresome old lady, who prided herself on having the goods on everyone. She said Bethany and her kids were renting the upper part of a duplex from a Mexican landlady, whose name was *Olivia* something.

"Olivia's no kin to that little Ramón, but all those Mexicans know each other. Thick as thieves. That Bethany's a great one for cussin'. Once I heard her swearin' at Olivia and Olivia swearin' back—cussin' in two languages. And that older girl . . . I won't repeat what she called her little sister, but it starts with a *c* and ends with a *t*."

"It's a pity," Howard said.

"The social workers came three times I know about, and God knows how many more. Bethany still sleeps with the little one's father, even after he walked out on her. I don't trust any of those kids, especially the little Mexican."

"Ramón? He seems okay," he said though he thought the kids were all out for the main chance. Clark had said he suspected Bethany's kids of swiping stuff last year. But the old lady annoyed him. As a little kid, he'd been a sneak thief too, had lifted mints from his grandfather's candy dish after the old man went blind.

One day when Mrs. Chick was working nearby, Howard saw the four coming back up the alley with two Mexican kids about the age of Ennis and Shannon. They were in the middle of an argument about someone messing with someone else's PlayStation controller.

"You was leaning into me," said the younger cousin, a chubby kid in a Mighty Mouse shirt, who clenched and unclenched his fists as he danced around Ennis.

"No way did I lean," said Ennis.

"Did so. Did so."

"You're full of shit," said Madison to the cousins.

"Hey, can it. You're in public here," Howard said.

"From now on none of you can use the PlayStation. I swear on my uncle's grave," said the older cousin.

Ramón hopped up and down, shrieking, "Goddamnit, how come? Goddamn you assholes to hell!"

Mrs. Chick stabbed the end of her long-handled weeding tool into the ground. "All you kids go home before I call the police. I will not have such language on my street. I won't have it."

Madison brushed hair back from her red face. "This is a public street. Howard just said so."

"What I meant was you have to be considerate. What you're fighting over isn't worth a hill of beans."

Mrs. Chick screwed her face into a sneer and said, "I'm good friends with the chief of police, and I'll have you all removed. Tell your mother I've lived on this street a lot longer than her."

The kids said no more, but when the old lady wasn't looking, Madison gave her the finger.

The next day the kids had forgotten the fight, but Howard lectured them on being nicer to Mrs. Chick. "You have to learn to get along with all kinds of people."

"Tell *her* that," Ennis said.

It wasn't like Howard was any great role model, but at least he could grow tomatoes better than old Clark. When his nephew dropped by the garden one day, Howard said he wouldn't mind staying on longer than the two months. He could use the exercise.

Often Ignatz would stumble over to join him, sleepy-eyed, carrying his bowl of cereal. Together they staked and tied the tomatoes and, because of Howard's careful watering, the vines grew like crazy and soon had golf-ball-size fruit. "Ignatz," he said, "See what thou hast wrought!"

"What're you saying?"

"Look what you grew, Ignatz! What you grew!"

Often the boy was silent. Other times he talked a blue streak, rambling on about whatever was on his mind, and he'd forget what he was doing and pull up radishes in Howard's plot or knock over the hyacinth-bean tepee.

One day the boy ran through his list of fathers, beginning with his real dad, Ennis Jenkins Sr., whom he barely remembered. When he was five, there had been a guy named Forrest Colton. "Forrest was an old bald guy. He watched monster truck shows and hollered like crazy."

The next dad was Keith. "He was African-American. Keith could pay the guitar better than that other Keith, you know, in the Rollin' Stones.

"Old Forrest'd peel off his belt and give it to us. We couldn't play with none of his stuff. He had a collection of metal trucks and stuff up on a shelf. Once I took one down, but I forgot to put it back. I got a bad whippin'. He had over a hundred he collected in truck stops."

Ennis shrugged as if to say things came and went, good and bad. You couldn't take it too seriously.

"Keith was a lot better, but then his mother got sick, and he left, and then it was Big Ramón."

"How long was Keith around?"

"I don't know. Maybe two years. He made us a garden. We had huge tomatoes all summer. Cantaloupes. Everything you can grow in a garden, we had it."

"Everything?"

"Yeah. Onions, peppers, tomatoes, watermelons, cantaloupes, radishes, corn, everything."

Howard almost asked, "Then how is it you didn't recognize kohlrabi?" but said, "You can't beat a big garden."

Ennis took home the first peppers and tomatoes, and one day his mother came over to thank Howard. From a distance, her weight made her look older, but up close you could see she was probably early thirties at best, a baby-faced woman with hooded eyes wearing an orange tank, Bermuda shorts, and flip-flops

She stared at the okra plants and said in a shy voice, "I sure want to thank you. You been a blessin' to my kids."

"Thank you, ma'am." He saw she wanted to keep the bounty coming. But maybe there was a particle of sincerity somewhere.

When she got over her shyness, she proved to be a rambling, self-preoccupied talker. "My mother use to fix fried okra," she said. "Nothing better. She cooked it with onions and peppers and what have you. It was the peppers made it good, but sometimes she made it with hot peppers, and I'd say, *Ma, I can't eat it thataway.* I always had a sensitive stomach since I was a kid. Never did like chicken nor pork. The smell gets to me every time."

Howard was down on his painful knees, weeding.

"Smells are my weakness. Oil smells gag me. Sometimes, if I'm riding in a car with the windows down, the pollution makes me so sick I could puke. Now, skunk don't bother me too bad, but mothballs does. Chemicals. If get a whiff of ammonia, I about die."

On and on. He struggled to his feet and said it was time to be getting home. As he drove off, he watched Bethany haul herself up her front steps. Her heavy hair hung down her back. Why hadn't she thought to put it up?

Poor Ignatz. Poor little kid. It was a wonder he didn't brain her with a brick.

Later that week he got an earful of what Mrs. Chick had talked about. Bethany was out on the porch, and you could hear her clear across the street, having it out with someone. "You said you was gonna fix it, but you never done shit. How are me and my kids supposed to live in this fuckin' dump?"

In mid-July temperatures stayed fairly moderate, and there were several nice rains. Ennis and Howard pushed the bamboo poles supporting the flourishing hyacinth bean vines deeper, and the tepee stayed upright when Ennis knocked into it. Fuchsia flowers opened. The kids didn't play inside the tepee as Howard had pictured though Shannon did venture inside for half a minute and pronounce it a *pretty thing*.

Ennis peered out from an opening in the tepee and said, "I wish I could be a Indian. They had super big bows and arrows." An hour later, Howard saw him and the older half cousin running around barefoot, shooting at a squirrel under a car with a BB gun. Howard walked across the street and took the gun from Ennis. "You can't be running around with a loaded gun, Ignatz. There'll be hell to pay. Mrs. Chick'll call the cops."

"Old bitch." The squirrel made a dash across the street and up a tree.

"That's not nice talk. Anyway, if you're going to shoot, why don't you set up a target in the backyard so things don't go haywire? Forget squirrels. They want to live." But when he was a kid, he had shot at squirrels, birds, rabbits, the usual things boys went after.

"Keith used to let me shoot at sparrows. They drive my mother nuts. Chip, chip, chip all day long. I can help with your weeding. Two bucks."

Howard guessed Bethany had put him up to asking. "You'll soon be getting some ripe tomatoes. Sell those if you want."

"How much do you think I can get?"

A day or so after the gun business, Bethany revisited the garden with Shannon. While Shannon sat on a bench with her legs stuck out, Bethany related all that was wrong with her landlady, whom she called *Livie* and sometimes *Dipshit*. "They finally got my air conditioner fixed, but it took Dipshit two whole days. And she forgot about the kitchen faucet, and I'm paying for water down the drain."

The woman was extremely irritating. "Maybe you're supposed to keep up repairs," he said. "Look at your contract."

"I don't hardly have a man around. Big Ramón was okay until six months after Little Ramón; then he stopped supporting us. He only comes around when he wants *you know*."

"*You know* must be your middle name, huh?"

"You got a way of makin' up names for people, don't you?"

"I'm clever that way."

"Clever is as clever does."

"What's that mean?"

"Take it or leave it."

"Jesus H. Christ." He went back to weeding.

But when he thought about it, he felt bad about the *you-know* business. She was a lamebrain, but maybe she couldn't entirely help herself, and she did have it rough.

He picked some of his just-reddening tomatoes and a few early peppers, lugged himself up the steps to Bethany's cluttered porch, and knocked on the screen door. The living room was a total wreck with old pillows and blankets strewn about. The remains of last night's pizza were congealing in a box in front of Madison, who lay on the couch talking on a lavender cell phone.

Bethany stared at him through the screen. "That stuff for me?"

"Hey Bethany, I'm sorry I made that comment yesterday. That was uncalled for, so I hope you'll accept my apology."

"Okay, sure. What the hell."

"Where's Ig . . . ? Where's Ennis this morning?"

"In time out. He got into it with Shannon. They was rolling around on that rug you're standing on."

He looked down. The rug was a faded thing with cabbage roses in the middle, some old person's castoff.

"Can he give me a hand?"

"I guess." Ennis stumbled out, sleepy and more hangdog than Howard had ever seen him, so skinny and pathetic in his undershorts, rail thin.

"You look like you could use some sleep, Ignatz?"

"I'm hungry. Can I have a waffle?"

"You know where they are." Bethany gave Howard a look that said, *See, my kids don't get away with anything,* as if fixing the boy a frozen waffle was an indulgence. Howard knew that look. Last week a toddler sitting in the grocery cart in front of him had grabbed the bar that separates people's groceries, and his mother had slapped his hand. The message was: *I've got things under control. No disrespect is called for*.

Ennis went into the kitchen and opened the refrigerator door. The fridge was bare inside except for a large jar of peanut butter, a sack of bread, a bag of something green, and an uncovered bowl of macaroni and cheese. It occurred to Howard he could have been taking snacks to the kids all along. Why hadn't he thought of it?

When he cashed his garden-steward check, he went back to see Bethany. "Listen, Kiddo," he said, handing her a fifty, "it seems you're kind of struggling what with the air conditioner and all. Here's something to buy groceries with." He handed her a twenty as well. "Ennis helped me a lot. Consider he earned it."

"Well, thank you, Howard. Heaven sent you to us. You're our angel." She said she'd gone to two food pantries and only netted some day-old bread and a mess of greens. They had told her to come back for family counseling, but *duh, what about the taxi*? She looked up at him. He handed her another twenty.

⎯⎯◇⎯⎯

"She's borderline negligent," Clark said when Howard asked if Clark could help get the family more assistance. "I can put in a word," Clark said. "I feel for those kids, especially that skinny older boy. What's his name?"

"Ennis. I call him *Ignatz*."

Clark laughed. "So does that make you Krazy Kat, Uncle Howard? You love that little kid?"

"L'il ainjil," Howard said. "Nah, the whole family's on the take. Oh, hell, he's a good kid."

With his own money squeeze, he didn't know how long he could continue his role as *garden angel*, as Bethany put it, grinning at her great witticism. Obviously, she'd coached the kids to call him *Uncle Howard* when the ice cream truck was in the vicinity. Madison asked for ten bucks, "so we can buy us some good hamburger meat, not that cheap stuff that clogs your pores."

He handed it over. "Buy lean," he said. "Check the label."

Howard bought them each a book though he suspected it was hopeless since they'd grown up with TVs stapled to their umbilicals, but Ramón actually read *James and the Giant Peach* and said it was "awesome when the peach gets stuck on that pole on top of the Empire State Building." Howard had thought Ennis might go for a Wimpy Kid book since his youngest grandson had loved the series, but Ennis said, "I saw the movie. All that *Cheese Touch* shit. I'd never fall for none of that."

"In my opinion books are better than movies nine times out of ten" Howard said.

"How can they be? Movies gots bigger pitchers. No book can have pitchers that big. They'd have to haul it around in a damn truck."

"How come you're not smiling when you say that? Okay, have it your way. Be illiterate. Join the rest of Americans. Can't read, can't think. Believe what you hear on TV. Come on, boy. I know you're smarter than that."

"Are you married?"

"I was, but my wife died, for your information."

"What'd she die of?"

"Heart disease. I don't want to talk about it, so don't ask questions."

"What if you married my mom? You could make her get smarter. You're old, but who cares?"

"Didn't anyone ever teach you manners? But you're right. I'm old, and she's young, and anyway we wouldn't get along."

"Well, think about it. I ain't said nothing yet."

"Don't. Promise me."

"All right." Ennis thought a minute. "It probably wouldn't work because she don't like you all that much."

"How come?"

"Says you look like an old bear."

"Grizzly or polar?"

"She said a bear."

He hadn't the slightest intention of getting the least bit closer to Bethany. The day he'd given them money for hamburger, Madison had brought him over a grilled burger on a bun. "Not much good," she grumbled. "It's 93% lean. Got no juice. But Mom wanted you to have it, Uncle Howard." That made him nervous.

But he was a doofus, like his nephew, and he thought of Ennis's proposition, but only for a moment, which took place at three in the morning, a time when his thoughts zinged around like bats. Was there anything to be said for Bethany? Well, she was a survivor. So what? People always talked about survivors as if they were saints, but more often than not people survived by using other people.

Was she at all attractive? She was a chunk, and sweaty, but she had pretty skin though she was freckled. Actually, the freckles were kind of sweet. Her hair, when it was clean, was a shiny red brown. But she had a totally untrained brain. It was a royal pain the way she rattled off clichés, her versions anyway. "Do I look like I just rolled off the turnip truck?" she'd say.

"No, Bethany," he'd say, "you look like you fell off the rutabaga truck."

She thought everyone had cheated her, was about to cheat her, or would cheat her in the future, including him. Considering all these things in the early morning, he would pull the pillow over his head and moan.

In August, after their Pick-Two lunch, he invited Milt to follow him to the garden. It looked pretty damn good if he did say so. He'd paid the kids a little to help weed and wanted to show it off, the kids as well. He'd almost said *my kids* though he knew Milt might not think highly of Madison or Shannon or even little Ramón. Since Howard had begun supplying them with granola bars, it looked like Ignatz might have gained a pound. He'd grown very tan over the summer since he went shirtless so much. Howard had taken him and Ramón to the barber for haircuts, and both came out looking spiffy. He was proud of them, almost as if they were his grandkids— well, grandkids in need of attention. Hadn't Milt bragged about his grandson who was autistic but smart as a whip?

When they arrived at the garden, Ennis was on his front porch. "Come meet my old friend here," Howard called. "He was on a farm team for the Royals once."

The kid took his time ambling across the street. "I've been waiting for you to show up," he said. "The Royals gots a farm?"

"Not quite." Milt stuck a piece of gum in his mouth. "It was the Kansas City A's back then."

"Royals, A's, same thing," said Howard.

"I never heard of them," said Ignatz, unimpressed. He whipped out a Lexibook console Howard had just bought him at Best Buy.

"Cute kid," Milt said when Ignatz headed home. "But not educated. Country kid?"

"Sharp as a tack." He handed Milt some of his best tomatoes to make up for the thought that Milt was a numbnuts, who didn't know potential when he saw it. "A whiz at Sudoku."

Only a week later, things heated up between the family and the landlady. Howard had met Olivia and thought her sensible enough. It would be damn hard under any circumstances to have a family living upstairs, especially one with four noisy kids though, come to think of it, Madison might not make much of a ruckus. She always looked as if she had a hard time keeping herself upright. Gravity was pulling on her as it was her mother. The girl was getting fatter. She was always flirting with the ice cream guy, trying to get a second scoop free.

The lot of them—from skinny Ennis and Shannon to slouchy Madison to sharp-eyed Ramón, who spent his time lighting firecrackers from the arsenal he'd acquired in July by wheedling or stealing—all seemed doomed to grow up semiliterates or con artists or both. They all needed an infusion of cash for special camps, dentists, tutors, barbers, psychologists, and allergists. Shannon wheezed.

He was too old, and his resources were limited, but when Clark told him about a soccer camp for inner-city kids, he paid for the boys. Ramón thrived, but Ennis refused to return when someone called him a hillbilly.

"Ignatz, you can't be a quitter. How're you going to get ahead in life?"

"I'm going to sell my vegables. Each year I'm going to make my garden bigger. Next year, I'm growing watermelons. Screw the dumb okra. You help me start something big over there in the back." He pointed to the duplex.

"Okay, Ignatz. Count me in. We'll keep in touch in the winter, okay?"

But another month went by, and Olivia got fed up and threw them out. One day Howard was standing in the garden, noticing purple seed pods on the hyacinth bean vines when Ennis, Madison, and Shannon, Bethany too, came walking down the front steps, carrying trash bags and suitcases. The kids carried backpacks as well. They passed without speaking and headed toward the alley. He had a tight feeling in his chest.

"Where are you all going?"

"Bus stop down the street," Ignatz said. "Going to the Greyhound station. We have to move back to Arkansas. They got a place down there for us since we can't live at Olivia's." He sneered over his shoulder at the duplex behind him.

"You can't stay at your cousins' place?"

"Full up," said Madison.

"Olivia said she'd call the cops," Bethany said. She was red-faced and weeping. Ennis and his sisters looked straight ahead.

"Where's Ramón?" Howard asked.

"With Big Ramón," said Madison. "Just for a while."

"What about your garden?" he asked Ennis. "It's doing so well. You can't leave it."

"Give it to the next guy. I probably won't be back."

"You can't work something out? Do you want me to talk to Olivia? I will if you want me to." He felt the wind had been knocked out of him. "Let me write down your phone number at least. Give me a call when—"

"We don't have a phone yet," Bethany said.

"I'll call the social worker. Who is it? Here, take my number." He scrawled it on a piece of paper and handed it to Ennis, who wadded it up and stuffed it in his pocket.

"I'll call. I'm glad to call somebody." Howard's voice sounded weak, winded.

"Sure, try," Madison said, "But it won't work. The caseworker already talked to her on the phone. Conflict resolution. She said *no way*."

It was only about eighty, but the day was very humid, following last night's thunderstorm. Bethany and the kids walked past him, and before he knew it, they were halfway down the alley, approaching the overflowing water holes where birds splashed, oblivious to what had just taken place. The growth appeared to have thickened overnight. It seemed to Howard the four of them were like a sad little band of explorers about to enter a jungle, carrying suitcases.

He watched the girls avoiding and Ignatz marching through the pools of water. Bethany turned left and disappeared into an opening in the brush, and one by one the others followed.

Acknowledgments

"Dead Duck"—*The Dalhousie Review*

"Religious Advisers"—*The Same*

"Butterfly Man"—*Nimrod* as "The Butterfly Man"

"Biker"—*Chariton Review*

"Adventures in Learning"-*Rosebud*

"The Garrs" *New Letters*

"Brighton Green"—*Miranda Literary Magazine*

"Ignatz"—*Cottonwood*

I want to thank my family and friends for their support; the Collaborators and the Diversifiers, who have provided encouragement, friendship, and good writing advice for many years; Gary Lechliter, Maryfrances Wagner, Greg Field, Brian Daldorph, the late Phil Miller, Nancy Eldridge, Bob Stewart, and Sylvia Kofler for publishing my stories; friends/readers Kris Huffman, Rob Vuturo, Mary Siegfried, Tom Weis, Don and Kathy Caswell, Jason Vaughan, and my late friends and supporters, JoAnn Nelson, Virginia Schneider, Janet Klaas, Janice Atkins, Conci Deniston, and Elaine Lally. I wish there were a way to send the last six and Phil a copy of the book. I would also like to thank BkMk Press for publishing *Odd Ducks* and Ben Furnish and Cynthia Beard for their gentle, careful editing and book design.

Patricia Lawson's work has appeared in *Pleiades*, *Dalhousie Review*, *New Letters*, and elsewhere. She taught for many years at Kansas City Kansas Community College and was an associate editor of *The Same*. She is a Riverfront Readings committee member at the Writers Place in Kansas City and a graduate of the University of Missouri-Kansas City. *Odd Ducks* is her solo fiction debut.

BkMk Press is grateful for the support it has recently received from the following organizations and individuals:

Miller-Mellor Foundation
Neptune Foundation
Richard J. Stern Foundation for the Arts
Stanley H. Durwood Foundation
William T. Kemper Foundation

Beverly Burch
Jaimee Wriston Colbert
Maija Rhee Devine
Whitney and Mariella Kerr
Carla Klausner
Lorraine M. López
Patricia Cleary Miller
Margot Patterson
Alan Proctor
James Hugo Rifenbark
Roderick and Wyatt Townley